THE COWBOY BARGAIN

A CANYON SPRING NOVEL

S.M. WEST

KIMBERLY QUINN

Edits: Happily Editing Anns
Cover Design: KiWi Cover Design Co.
Photography: Wander Aguiar
Model: Andrew Biernat

Welcome to Prospect, Montana, and the Kincaide family. Here's all the siblings and their stories to come. They are listed in order of their ages, not the release of their books:

THE COWBOY BARGAIN

A bargain with an expiration date and we both get what we want.
That's what I agreed to. That's what he promised.

Brooks Kincaide.

Rude.
Cocky.
And far too sexy for his own good.

He's now my husband—even if our union is fake and our families hate each other.

Our deal helps us both.
No strings. No sex. And no falling in love.
We're strictly business.
I save my ailing ranch and Brooks takes control of Canyon Spring—his rightful legacy.

But we soon realize we have more in common than boiling family tensions and a shared property line.
I can't stop thinking about him, and though I pretend not to like it, every time he calls me darlin', I get weak in the knees.

Now the lines between business and marriage blur, and that's when everything falls apart.

I should have known better than to make a deal with a
Kincaide.
Or more like the devil.

Because I stand to lose not only my ranch, but also my heart.

1

BROOKS

"The devil is dead." My sister slides her arm from the crook of mine with a hint of a smile in her whispered voice.

Scarlett's always had a sharp tongue, and we all grieve differently, but even for her this seems melodramatic. I send her a pointed look.

"What? You're thinking it, too." She brushes her elegantly manicured fingers across the shoulder of my suit. "Brooks, don't even try to deny it."

"Scarlett." My tone is as gentle as my hands when I cup her elbows to stop her pointless fussing. "You don't mean that."

"Oh, don't I? The man was ruthless." She tucks a raven strand of hair behind her ear and glances around the room. "Impossible to love."

We're in the largest conference room of Butler and Associates, where a dozen tufted red leather chairs encircle the table. Yet, it feels more like a hunting lodge than a law firm, with its rustic wood carvings, a deer's head on one wall and a full-sized bear in the corner.

I've been in this place countless times and would have been here when Pa died, if only he'd taken me to his meeting that day, instead of keeping secrets.

Maybe if I'd been here...

Shaking away those dark thoughts, I lock eyes with my sister's ocean blues, so like mine. She can try to hide it, but she's hurting. We all are. In our own ways.

Sadly, we've all been at the mercy of Devlin Kincaide, father of eight, adopted father of one, rancher to thousands, a pillar of the Prospect community, and revered owner of Canyon Spring Ranch.

Scarlett more so than others.

No matter how hard she tried, she never could please him, and I can't blame her for lashing out. But Pa's only been gone a month and her callous comments sound an awful lot like him.

"Don't look at me that way." She pulls out two chairs as Jett, her twin, enters the room. "All of us bent over backward for that man. You most of all..." At the sight of Jett and Jasper, the youngest of nine, talking across the room, her voice trails off as if she's run out of steam.

Grateful for her divided attention and my opportunity to drop this painful subject, I turn, only to stop midway when she picks up right where she left off.

"You sacrificed the most and always for the good of the family and ranch. Pa knew it, but it was still never enough.

It's okay to admit there's a bit of joy mixed with your grief. It's understandable. Human even."

"It isn't like that. I'd do anything for Canyon Spring. For us. I find no pleasure in—"

"Shhh." Her palm runs over my suit once again and her unwavering gaze softens.

We don't need words to express our shared loss because, despite the ill-timing, I can't deny most of what she's said is true.

"He was bullheaded, unpredictable, and fickle at times, but he loved you." I gently kiss the top of her head.

"Hey, what did I miss?" Jett sidles up to us, knocking shoulders with his twin.

"Nothing." Scarlett's dismissive, pulling him to the chairs she set aside. "We're waiting on Mama, Trey, and Ridge."

They tuck into their seats, dark heads together, whispering in hushed tones like when they were kids, and my lips curve upward at the sight. Even as adults, they're an inseparable duo.

Charlie Butler, our family lawyer since I was in diapers, stands at the far end of the room. On my way to greet him, I share a look with my brother Cole, the life of any party and my closest ally, then Laken, the apple of Pa's eye. Her nose is red tipped, expression grim, and it's clear she's not coping well. Still, she doesn't seek comfort—she's too proud, and too much like Pa to admit she needs it.

"Brooks, it's good to see you." Charlie clamps a firm yet aged hand on my shoulder. "I sure wish it was under different circumstances. How are you doing?"

How *am* I doing? It's a damn good question.

With Pa's passing, I'm faced with uncertainty and sadness...yet, deep down, some relief.

As his firstborn, I did everything in my power to gain his approval. To win his trust. Perhaps even earn his respect. All in the hope I'd one day fill his shoes and take my rightful place as head of the ranch.

It's everything I've worked for and all I've ever wanted. And now, at thirty-seven, it'll finally be mine. I just never wanted or imagined it would come at the expense of his life.

It's bitter-fucking-sweet.

Of course, I can't say any of this to Charlie.

"I think we've all been better, but at least after today we can move on with business..."

He drops my gaze and glances to the doorway as Sage Kincaide, my mother, enters the room.

I'm struck by how beautiful she is, even widowed and grieving. Dressed in black with her platinum-blonde hair swept off her face and her makeup done in that modest way she has, she's understated grace.

Trey flanks her side, his perpetual spot. Not that he's a suck up, more like her guard dog. He's a cousin, adopted by my parents as a baby, and I've always wondered if his loyalty to Mama is out of obligation—some kind of debt for taking him in—or if it's genuine.

Ridge, the second eldest, enters the room and closes the door behind him. He's the last to take a seat. Now, we can begin.

We're all here except Clay, but since he refused to come for the funeral, Mama made it clear he wouldn't be welcome today.

I guess now that he's a chart-topping country singer, family isn't his priority.

Truthfully, it doesn't shock me. Of all the siblings, he had the hardest time dealing with Pa. He hightailed it out of Prospect at his first opportunity, and never looked back.

Thoughts about my famous, wayward brother are dispelled when Charlie starts reading, "I, Devlin Kincaide of Prospect, in the state of Montana, being of sound mind, hereby declare this is my last will and testament."

He lists the family ranch home, investments, and bank accounts. All the major assets are left to Mama, as expected.

"As for the overall management of Canyon Spring Ranch..."

I straighten in my seat, ready to be named my father's successor, as Charlie pauses to glance around the table, making eye contact with everyone.

Everyone *but* me.

After a weighted silence, he clears his throat. "I hereby name my second son, Ridge, as head of all ranch operations, business and otherwise. Ridge, this appointment is conditional on your marriage, within six months from today, to a woman of equal or greater standing to the Kincaides, and who must be approved by your mother, my beloved wife, Sage."

Invisible flames lick my overheated skin and sweat trickles down my back.

This can't be happening.

But Charlie presses on, as though this was perfectly predictable. "Should these conditions not be met, Sage will determine who is best to run the ranch."

I can't believe...Ridge? In charge?

Fuck. Why am I surprised?

When we were little, we were inseparable, and this irked Pa to no end. He wanted to make us men, even at ages five and three. Men weren't soft and they sure as shit didn't have best friends.

At the time, I didn't see it—the poisoning of our bond. I was too young and too eager to please. And Pa? Well, I've no doubt he enjoyed every second of pitting his sons against one another.

Everything was a competition, from who learned to ride first and who did it best, to who was the best wrangler, the best shooter...the best goddamn son. It never ended.

Even now—dead and gone—he's still playing us against each other. Enemies even.

I should be used to it. Hell, I should have expected nothing less.

Still, it stings.

Like a son of a bitch.

"To my eldest son, Brooks." Finally, Charlie has the balls to look at me. "I expect your full support of Ridge in all Canyon Spring endeavors. Ranching is in your blood, but..." He pauses and the hand holding the will rattles as he does his throat clearing thing again. "But you aren't a leader..."

His words fade, replaced by my thundering heart, and a numbness washes over me like a wet, heavy blanket, blocking out the noise. If only it would erase the furtive, curious, and slack-jawed glances from those around the table.

They look stunned.

All of them, except Mama, whose piercing blue eyes bore

into mine with cold determination—not an ounce of surprise in her stare.

I'm suddenly hit with the urge to run. But I won't.

I refuse to give Mama, Ridge, and perhaps even the ghost of Devlin Kincaide the satisfaction.

Charlie drones on, his voice more an incessant buzz than specific words. My mind runs in circles, chased by old wounds and pent-up emotions.

It seems, even in the end, the asshole got the best of me.

Everyone knows what I gave up for him. For the ranch. For my family.

God, all the shit I swallowed.

My hands are filthy from the things I did without question, even when I had my doubts and hated every second of it. Even when it was wrong, I did it.

And for what?

"You all right?" Cole's voice breaks me out of my stupor.

The meeting has ended. We're alone now—thank fuck—but I can't face him.

I growl, turning my head from his pitying gaze. "I can't believe..."

Cole and I are ten years apart, yet we're close. He's the only one who values my advice even if he doesn't often follow it. Half the time, I'm getting him out of one mess or another, like saving him from a beating when he was caught with his pants down and his dick inside a married woman.

I'm a failure. How can I look him in the eye? Hell, how can I face anyone? I never saw this coming.

If Devlin Kincaide were here today, I'd beat the shit out of him.

"Hey, c'mon." He tries to pry me from the chair. "Let's get out of here."

Standing, I tear from his grip and push the chair with such force that it smashes into the wall behind me. "This is fucking bullshit! I've got what it takes to run the ranch better than anyone else."

"Whoa, take it easy." Alarmed, he holds his hands up in front of him, moving slowly as if trying to tame a wild mustang. "It is a very large pile of shit. We'll get through it. Let's just—"

"I've gotta get out of here." I charge for the door, and Cole, muttering his agreement, follows.

Outside the room, I nearly run into Charlie. How long did he know that I never stood a chance of running things? Pa must have confided in him—he told him everything else about the business, for fuck's sake. He must think I'm a joke.

Acid burns in the pit of my stomach. But I've got no beef with him. It wasn't his decision. He was only doing his job.

"Charlie." Barely containing my rage, I dip my head and push through the doors, inhaling the sweet Montana air.

The day is warm with the sun high and bright in the pale blue sky. But even nature's beauty can't lighten my foul mood. The storm inside me only darkens as I stand not even twenty feet from where my father dropped dead on the sidewalk.

I would have been with him that day if he hadn't cut me out and taken Ridge instead.

Until today, it was the worst day of my life. Not because he'd played his usual games and power trips—Ridge and I never knew which one of us would be his target—but because I'd lost my father. I'd never have another chance to make him proud.

Shit, Scarlett might be right—he really was the devil.

My family mills around outside, their chatter drying up when they spot me. Some gawk, others' expressions drown in sympathy or indifference, and some turn away.

Mama's expression is still stoic and impenetrable.

And Ridge? It may just be me, but I swear his chest puffs out when our gazes lock. He never misses a chance to gloat and saunters toward me with his politician's smile lighting his pretty boy face.

"Brooks, no hard feelings, I hope. I'm proud to have you as my second in command." He extends his hand as if I'll shake on this bullshit. "At least I know you can take orders."

That's it.

Last fucking straw.

Like a bucking bronco, I fly at him with my arms swinging, relishing the sweet crack of my fist against his jaw.

2

ADDISON

The cool shade of the house lingers at my back as I hop off our sagging front porch and saunter across the dusty stone path to the garage.

It's another gorgeous Montana day, with barely a cloud in the sky, and I wish I could relax and enjoy it. This free spirit wants nothing more than to laze beside the pond in my new two-piece, soaking up the sun with a beer in hand. Or a book. I'm not picky.

But free time is a luxury now that I'm involved in running our family cattle ranch.

When my father said he wanted me to take over operations, I knew it wasn't going to be easy. Still, I wasn't expecting it to be quite this hard.

The work is never-ending, and there aren't many hands to help do it. I wake up sore and tired, and I go to bed sore and tired. Heck, even in my dreams, I'm sore and tired.

Still, I love it.

"You heading into town?" Daddy sits like a king at the wheel of his truck with his arm propped on the open window and the brim of his hat pulled low.

It reminds me of how he used to look, saddled on his horse. He always seemed so large and imposing with his big black mustang under him and every cowboy on the ranch following his lead. I thought he was the smartest, most powerful man in the world. That nothing could ever unseat him. I believed as long as he was around, I'd be protected.

"I am," I confirm with a smile, ignoring the melodramatic squeeze of my heart, and try not to pine for all that's changed.

Daddy may still be with me, but the tables have turned. Now I'm the one protecting him, because no man is infallible, and nothing lasts forever.

Not even George Monroe.

"You off to see the new filly Hank brought in?" I ask, my chest still feeling tight.

"Sure am. I hear she's a wild one, and I figure he won't shut up about it 'til I get my old butt out to the stables and see her for myself."

"You expect *Hank* to be quiet?" I raise an eyebrow. "That man's mouth is almost as big as his ego. Actually...that seems to be a common trait around here. Describes most of the men on this ranch."

Daddy shakes his head, his shoulders lifting on a silent chuckle.

We both know my cousin Hank has been nothing but a godsend for us and our ranch. He came to help us after Daddy's first trip to the hospital and never left. Without him and the other hands working our ranch, we'd be in some deep trouble.

Deeper than we already are.

"Derek never stood a chance with you."

"Daddy!" I land my hands on my hips and hold my head high. If I don't at least fake offense, I'll never hear the end of his teasing.

"What? It's true and you know it." The lines around his mouth deepen, and he studies me with what might be a gleam of pride in his eyes. "I feel sorry for the next man who tries to wrangle you."

"Who says I can't be the one to do the wrangling?"

He slaps the side of his truck, a peel of raspy laughter lighting him up. "Yup. The next guy's doomed for sure," he wheezes.

He could be right, but I'm not up for discussing Derek or any of my other brief and somewhat disastrous relationships.

It's not my fault none of the men in our little town of Prospect have kept my interest long. Maybe if one of them had some character or saw me as something more than their next housekeeper—heck, if just one of them considered me an equal—things might be different.

"Guess that means you're stuck with me, old man." I stick out my tongue, giving him my usual sass.

"I wouldn't have it any other way."

"I'll see you back here later," I promise, turning toward my truck, but hesitate after only a step. "Hey, Daddy? I'd like to talk to you more about my sustainability ideas for the ranch. I really think there's a future in it. Maybe tonight at dinner?"

"Maybe." His voice turns flat, and the humor seeps from his expression. "Don't forget the fertilizer for your mama's flowers."

And just like that, my hopes for bringing our aging business into the twenty-first century are dismissed. Again.

"Of course not." I force a tight smile, my teeth grinding with the effort, and tap a finger to my temple. "Top of my mind."

I'm a shitty liar. My face always gives away exactly what I'm thinking, and my mouth's usually helping it along. But Daddy doesn't seem to notice.

"Good girl." He clears his throat, a moment of silent tension passing before he adds, "She'll be happy to see you taking such good care of 'em."

I turn my gaze to Mama's prized flower gardens and hold back the sudden rush of emotion threatening to bring tears to my eyes.

She's been gone so long I hardly remember her. Sometimes, I'll catch a whiff of her perfume or feel a shadow of her soft arms around me and wonder where she is. What she's doing. If she's even still alive.

My memories of her are so faded, I don't even trust they're real.

They're certainly not welcome. I don't have room to care about a woman who abandoned her husband and eleven-year-old daughter. A woman who fled in the middle of the night, without a word or even a note to explain herself.

Twenty-one years later and we still don't know why. Probably never will.

But I've kept her damn flowers growing—the sea of red,

white, and blue petals blooming as bright as the day she first planted them. Not for her, or even for me, but for Daddy, who still talks like she's coming home tomorrow.

The sound of crunching gravel has me looking back to see him driving away, his hand held in the air in a goodbye salute.

I shield my eyes and watch the stubborn fool drive off, leaving my dreams in his dust.

Dammit. Why won't he listen?

In a fit, I kick at the gravel, sending tiny stones skittering in all directions and scuffing the toes of my boots.

It's childish, I know. But I'd be willing to sign a deal with the devil for a single solar panel if it would convince Daddy to go along with my sustainability plan. One panel's not near enough, but it's a heck of a lot better than what I've got now, which seems like nothing more than a sustainability pipe dream.

"Wants me to take over but won't let me actually do it," I mumble, climbing into my truck and heading for town.

I don't stop grumbling until my wheels hit pavement.

Yes, my pride's a bit hurt. And yes, part of me yearns to make him proud, to prove I'm as good a rancher as any man. But it's more than all that.

When Daddy's health started declining and the medical bills started rolling in, I learned how perilous our situation is.

On paper, the ranch is profitable, but start doing the math and soon enough you realize how thin that profit margin is. It doesn't take a genius to see the whole operation is only one bad season away from disaster. Starvation doesn't sound like a fun way to go, yet it's the direction we're headed.

My plan changes all that. Sustainable ranching is the future. Not only could it help save the planet, but it would also save Monroe Ranch from extinction and give Daddy the legacy he deserves.

But it's an expensive venture. One that's out of our reach without a business partner, and I know that's the thing holding Daddy back. He thinks partnering with someone means giving up control—something he's clearly not good with and a trait I *may* have inherited.

Yet if I could strike the right deal with the right partner, we could keep our ranch, keep our name, and keep everyone fed in the process. If I could find someone with money and influence. Someone who can see my vision and has the balls to follow a woman's lead.

Someone like a Kincaide.

Our neighbors at Canyon Spring Ranch aren't only the wealthiest, most influential family in our town of Prospect— possibly even the county—but they could also be the perfect solution to my problem. If I could convince them my plan's worth investing in, then Daddy would have no room to argue. With power like that backing me, he'd have no choice but to at least listen.

Except, because of an ancient feud over property lines and a fence, our families are sworn enemies. So, it's likely he'd disown me first and listen second.

The problem's still turning in my head when I finally roll into town.

Prospect looks the same as every other day. Same old

buildings. Same old people. Flowerpots line the store fronts, and signs welcome visitors to our historic town, which once was the boon of this area's gold rush. Legend says the town founder, Nestor Smith, picked a chunk of gold the size of an egg right off the ground on what's now the center of Main Street.

I have my doubts, but people have a way of turning fiction to fact in a town like this.

Nothing here ever changes, really.

Well, except the Golden Nugget bingo hall which still has the word *traitors* scrawled in neon pink across its brick exterior. A mystery vandal hit late last summer, after someone from our rival town, Golden Valley, won the jackpot.

Can't say for certain it was my granny Gertrude who did it, but rumor has it she returned to her room at the old folks' home with paint on her hands that night. That woman never could hold her temper.

No one turned her in, though. The people of this community are tight-knit. We may not always get along—like the Monroes and the Kincaides—but we respect and look out for each other. We're kind of like one big dysfunctional family that way.

It's midafternoon and I'm only here to run errands, but the bright red door of Ruby's tavern catches my eye.

"Fuck it." I make a sharp turn, slamming on the brakes and parking in front of the crimson door.

None of the men in my life would think twice about stopping for a midday drink, but as a woman trying to take charge, I find myself overthinking every decision. It's ridiculous. And exhausting.

"Hey, Addie!" Ruby greets over the noise of the old jukebox playing in the corner. "What can I get ya?"

I slide onto a rickety barstool and shoot her a weary smile. "I'll take a glass of that craft brew, if you've still got it."

"I sure do." Her reply is bright and bubbly, just like her personality and her enticing red door, but I don't miss the way her lips roll together or how she keeps sneaking glances my way as she pulls the tap.

"Go ahead and ask." I'm already guessing at what's on her mind.

The glass in her hand is full, but for some reason, she refuses to set it on the bar. Instead, she taunts me with it, leaning forward like she's about to spill a secret—or my damn beer—and whispers, "Is it true? You broke things off with Derek?"

I bite the inside of my lip to hold back my sigh.

While it's true, Derek and I are no longer a *thing*, I'd be lying if I didn't admit it bothers me just a teensy bit to know the whole damn town's flapping their gums about it. I nod, keeping my smile firmly in place.

"Well?" she urges, probably hoping for something juicy to share with her friends. "You going to tell me what happened?"

"There's really not much to tell."

Derek and I had a few good times, but they were fleeting. And while he's not bad to look at, his personality is about as engaging as the dusty wood panels covering the walls of this tavern. Also, there was that pesky problem of him wanting a real relationship and me...well, me not so much.

I shrug. "We want different things in life, I guess."

Ruby's laugh sounds more like a snort of contempt. "You mean you didn't want to be tied down to a man who's only interested in holding you back?"

"Yeah. All the men I've dated either want to change me, boss me, or rescue me. I've got no use for any of that."

"A man who wants any of that ain't much use to anyone."

She said it, not me. But still, I wonder sometimes. "I'm not sure any man has a hope with me, Ruby. I just don't think I'm relationship material."

"Oh, I wouldn't be so sure." Her eyes roam over my shoulder, and she finally puts the beer within my reach. "I think it just takes the right person."

The glass is cool when I snatch it up, and I smile for real, turning in my seat to see who or what has her attention.

My throat closes at the sight of Brooks Kincaide, sitting in the back corner booth with his head tilted and Adam's apple bobbing as he swallows his drink.

Well, fuck me sideways.

Now there is a man worth looking at. I could spend the day admiring his broad lines, shadowed jaw, and pop of cool blue eyes. If ever there were an example of physical male perfection, it's him.

A surge of adrenaline hits, and I bound off my stool, not spilling a drop of beer in the process. The answer to my problems is sitting just a few feet away.

He'd make the perfect business partner, no matter our family history. He's smart, dutiful, hardworking—a rancher, through and through. And now that Devlin's gone, Brooks is next in line to run the Kincaide empire.

Devlin was unapproachable—a scary sonofabitch—but

the man I'm admiring now isn't the same ruthless kind of creature. At least, he doesn't seem to be.

Before I even realize what they're doing, my feet carry me to the head of his table, my hands strangling my beer mug as heat crawls up the back of my neck.

But he doesn't even look my way, too busy staring at the bottom of his empty glass.

I clear my throat, hoping to make my intrusion a little less...intrusive. "Hey, Brooks."

When his piercing blues finally turn my way, they're red-rimmed, and the left one has a cut at the corner. Is it swollen? Has he been in a fight?

Not that it detracts from his appearance any. My gaze travels over his ruggedly handsome face to his wide shoulders and solid arms. His shirt sleeves are rolled, displaying thickly veined and muscled forearms. Dammit, even his hands are appealing.

Okay, especially his hands—bruised knuckles and all.

Heck, this man could grow a tail, and I'd probably still find him attractive. There's no two ways about it, Brooks Kincaide is hot.

"What the hell are you staring at?" he growls.

He's also a jackass. A big, hot jackass.

3

BROOKS

"B-r-rooks." Addison Monroe's lips pinch so tight she can barely get out my name.

What the hell is she doing here at my table? The Kincaides and Monroes steer clear of one another.

"We need to talk." She offers me a hesitant smile. Her long hair, the strange, eye-catching color of champagne, falls over her bare, sun-kissed shoulders.

"Not interested." I scowl and stare past her at Ruby behind the bar. "You got any of Hopper's moonshine?"

Ruby glares at me before walking through a door to the back.

Attagirl, she's got what I need.

"Don't you think you've had enough?" Addie tips her chin at the empty glasses and rests her beer on the table.

While Cole and I downed a shot of whiskey before he bailed, preferring the company of the ravishing redhead at the bar, I'm nowhere near done drowning my sorrows.

"I'm only getting started, and you're souring the mood." She isn't—I just don't feel much like talking.

In fact, Addie's a ray of sunshine amid the gloomy men in here, looking to get their drink on in the middle of the day.

Fuck, that includes me.

"Brooks, how many times have I told you not to go shooting your mouth off about Hop's moonshine." Ruby strolls over, voice lowered, and holds up a glass jug near filled with clear liquid. "It's only for my special customers."

I chuckle and slide both shot glasses to the edge of the table. "Aw, forgive me, Ruby. You know I meant no harm. Can't get moonshine like Hop's."

"Pshaw, you stop with that sweet talk, now." She pulls a bag of frozen peas from the front pocket of her apron and slaps it onto the table. "You look like you could use this."

"What's that for?" The sound of the cork popping tugs at the corners of my mouth and my sweet smile only gets bigger as she fills both glasses.

I down not one but two in succession, welcoming the fiery burn down my throat.

Ruby twists the corner of her wrinkled mouth. "Boy, you're going to hurt tomorrow. You better put that on your face, or the ladies aren't gonna think you're so pretty no more."

"Thanks, but I don't need that." I slide the cold peas toward her, numb from the alcohol, and hold up both glasses for a refill.

Regret may ride my ass tomorrow, but right now alcohol is the only remedy I need for the ache of my shiner and the senseless anger and disappointment whirling around in my head.

Today's for wallowing, and tomorrow...well, tomorrow I'll figure out how to snatch the head ranch position right from under Ridge's nose.

Smug son of a bitch.

"You're done, Brooks. No more." She stuffs the cork into the jug. "Do you have someone to take you home?"

"It's all right, Ruby, I'll make sure he gets home." Addie smiles and I growl. Who does she think she is? My keeper?

"I can take care of myself."

"Oh, you're doing a damn fine job." Sharp, sea-glass green eyes lock with mine.

"Well, I see you're in good hands." Ruby pats Addie's shoulder. "I'll just leave you two alone."

If I wasn't already seated, I'd be on the floor. Ruby walking away from a conversation is unheard of. That woman loves to gossip as much as the next person in this town, and a Kincaide and a Monroe talking...now, that's news.

I snort, shaking my head, and wince at the faint throb in my temple. As much as I hate to admit it, Ridge sure has a mean right hook. Almost as good as mine.

When he came at me after I got in a few good hits, the blow to my eye had me seeing stars. We might still be brawling if not for our brothers pulling us apart.

Now just the two of us, Addie steps closer, placing the cool, soft tips of her fingers on the skin around my eye. "What happened?"

Her touch causes my groin to heat, and the sweetest sensation unfurls in my chest.

Fuck.

"Nothing." The gruff word slips past my tight lips. "I don't need your pity. You're just like him. What do you know about having to prove yourself? You just flutter your pretty little lashes, and you get what you want."

She jerks back like I've slapped her, and I regret my tone but not what I said.

"What are you talking about? I'm just like who?" Taking another step away from the table, she fists her hands at her sides.

Addie's not hard to look at, not in the least. Tall, a little above average and lean, she's nonetheless curvy in all the right places, a fact made plain by how the top of her cornflower blue dress stretches slightly over her perky chest. The cotton clings to her abdomen and slender waist, falling to just above her knee.

"Forget about it." I scrub a hand roughly down my face, trying to erase thoughts of her long legs wrapped around me as I drive my cock deep inside her.

Maybe Ruby's right and I am drunk if sex and Addison Monroe are coming at me in the same thought. She's bad news and a terrible reminder of what I've never had.

Her father adores her and treats her as an equal. Pa may have hated George Monroe, but Monroe was the kind of father I wish I'd had.

"I'm thinking this was a bad idea. You're drunk." She spins on her well-worn cowboy boots, causing her dress to flare.

Fuck, her thighs are lean and toned, and I saw a flash of white. Her panties?

"I'm not drunk but whatever." She needs to leave before I do something I'll regret.

"I'm sorry for your loss. Losing a parent is hard and not something you ever really get over." Her eyes glisten, and I hold back a groan as she glances at me over her shoulder.

Please don't fucking cry. Her mother always seemed like a damn fine woman, and I get why she might still miss her all these years later. But the loss of Devlin isn't the same. From the little I saw and heard, her mother had a heart.

Changing her mind about leaving, she fully faces me once more, her hands resting on her trim waist. ""I guess what I'm trying to say is, grief doesn't give you the right to be a jackass. You could at least try to be respectful even if you're hurting."

"Darlin', I don't answer to you." I bring the glass of her still cold beer to my mouth and down the contents in three gulps, then release a satisfied "Ahhh."

"God, you really are an asshole." The corners of her lush lips curl down.

"Now, Addie, how unladylike."

"I came here with a business proposition, thinking you'd be the reasonable one in the family, but clearly, I'm talking to the wrong brother. Maybe I'll just take my plan to Ridge."

Once again, she's about to give me her back as she turns on her heel, but with a sniper's aim, my arm shoots out and grips her bicep. "Oh, no you don't, darlin'." I pull her to me. "If you've got business with the Kincaides, talk to me."

Her nostrils flare, cheeks flush, and eyes darken. "Let go of me, Brooks."

"I will if you're ready to talk." I slide back into the booth, bringing her with me. The scent of honeysuckle hits my senses.

"You make it sound like I've been playing. I've been ready." She tries to yank her arm away, but she isn't going anywhere.

"Go on."

"Well, have you ever thought about lessening your environmental footprint?"

"What? Sustainable ranching?" I straighten, surprised by the direction of the conversation, and she nods. "Darlin', we're cattle ranchers. No two ways about it, we're bad for the environment."

She sniffs, straightening her shoulders and, while not intentional, thrusts out her damn perfect tits. "Even so, it doesn't mean we don't have to bother trying to reduce our impact on the environment."

"It's an awful lot of trouble and expense." I'm playing devil's advocate. Green practices aren't new to me, and there are merits.

"True, but the costs..." She pauses, nibbling on her bottom lip, and I stare, urging her to go on. "There's a profit to be made. For both of us if we did this together."

My "*no*" weighs heavy and sharp on my tongue, but I hold it. For now. I've entertained the idea of bringing sustainable practices to Canyon Spring Ranch.

And while the outlay can be costly and at first, on paper, look like a losing proposition, if done properly, there's money to be had. I had planned to broach the topic with Pa but hadn't figured out how to get him past the price tag.

She proceeds to spell out a sustainable partnership, throwing in that the Monroe ranch could go it alone. I could call bullshit—the rumors are alive and well about how they have hit hard times—but I don't.

Addie's smart and onto something, but I'm not in a position to do anything about it.

"This is just wishful thinking. Forget about it." My buzz is now a thing of the past, my reality just a little too sobering.

"Why? Brooks, I saw your face. You can't fool me. You're interested."

"You're projecting." I smirk at the irritation sparking in her gaze.

"How about if we go small and try something on the small side...say, solar fences. And if it fails, you can walk away," she suggests, and I shake my head, not budging. "I don't understand. You never struck me as a stupid man."

"Insulting me isn't the way to get me to change my mind, darlin'."

"Quit calling me that." Her light brows knit together.

I lower my voice and lean in. "I like how it lights a fire in your eyes when I say it."

"Does not." A blush creeps up her neck.

"Does."

"I'm not talking about this." She hits her palm on the tabletop. "Back to my plan. Do you need a day to think on it?"

"No." I could just leave it at that, but I keep going. "I'm not in a position to make this kind of decision."

"Oh. So, is it like a family decision-making thing now?" She cocks her head to one side.

Damn, it would be so easy to just say yes and keep my fucking pride intact, but I can't lie to her. "No. Ridge has the final say."

I don't bother adding that I could go to him with her idea and try to get his agreement. In truth, he'd be all over it and take credit for it. I won't give him that. Sustainable practices are the way to go, and once I'm managing the ranch, I'll partner with Addie. But there's no point in telling her any of this now because it'll take time.

"Oh…" She shifts and her thigh rubs against mine, and I stifle a groan. "You could take this to Ridge, couldn't you?"

"I could, but I won't." My lips mash into a thin line.

"So, it's a no?" There's a strange gleam in her eyes almost daring me to pass, but something is missing. There isn't a hint of defeat to her demeanor.

"Yeah." I exhale a long breath, the weight of the day sitting on my chest like a bull.

"Okay. I'll talk to Ridge, then." She leaps from the seat, and I'm on her like a fly on shit, grabbing her by the waist.

She lets out a tiny gasp, and I whisper, my lip grazing the shell of her ear. "No."

My chest is at her back, my head dipped low so I can see her face as she juts out her chin and narrows her eyes. "You can't stop me."

Even in my arms, not able to go anywhere, she's undeterred. Her sheer determination sparks a wild and crazy idea. One I've been mulling over since leaving the lawyer's office earlier today.

Although, at the time, I'd been without a woman in mind for the harebrained scheme. It may be the craziest and stupidest thing I've ever done but hell, why not?

"If you want this so bad, let's make a deal that'll get us both what we want."

"I'm listening." She arches a brow, and I turn her to face me.

Addison Monroe is a woman of equal standing to the Kincaides. Like me, ranching is as much a part of who she is as her bones, muscles, and beating heart. And she strikes me as someone with the smarts and know-how to see the benefits of a solid bargain.

"Marry me."

"What?" Her eyes widen as does her mouth.

She tries to pull back, and my fingers sink into the tender flesh of her waist. "Marry me so I can head up Canyon Spring and you get your sustainability partnership."

It's all in my head, but my knees wobble and the earth shakes as Devlin Kincaide rolls over in his grave. I can't help but crack a huge grin and rush to explain the details of Pa's will and how if I meet his conditions before Ridge, Mama will see I'm the better choice to head the ranch and even with the will, we all know, she always has the final say.

She makes a clean break from my hold. "I don't want to marry anyone."

"But don't you see...that's perfect." I inch closer, inhaling her intoxicating subtle, flowery scent.

"Perfect?" She cocks a hip. "You're delusional. I understand how this helps you and in a roundabout way, me. But what's to stop me from just going to Ridge with my plan? No marriage needed."

"You could, but he'll turn you down."

"You don't know that."

"Yeah, I do, and he'll take your idea as his own. Ridge isn't the partnering type. He'll beat you at your own game." I shut my mouth, giving her a chance to think.

There it is again, a fiery flash in her eye, and I know we're getting married.

4

ADDISON

"Fine, I'll marry you." The words are clear and fully formed and somehow make it past the sudden dryness of my throat, even though I can't believe I'm the one saying them.

I swallow hard as his eyes search mine, and my thirst grows deeper. Where's Ruby for a refill when you need her?

"Well, okay—"

"Not so fast," I blurt, hoping to say what I need before my throat closes up completely. "I've got conditions."

"Of course, you do." His gaze drops to my lips, and then lower, and lower still. "I'd expect nothing less from a girl like you."

A girl like me?

A girl like me?

"I'm a fully grown woman, thank you very much, but I'm going to pretend you didn't just speak to me like I'm some kind of pampered princess." I cross my arms over my chest, aiming for fierce but feeling utterly exposed.

His eyes snap back to mine. "Sorry, darlin'. It wasn't intentional."

I can't tell if he's giving me a line of bullshit or being freakishly sincere. Either way, I won't press him on it. At least, not right now.

"If we do this—if we get married—it's a business contract, nothing more. There can't be any blurred lines. That means I'm not cooking or cleaning for you, we're not having sex, and there will be no feelings involved. You absolutely cannot fall in love with me."

"Whoa, slow down a minute." He raises his arms in surrender, and he takes a step toward me like I'm some crazed wild thing he thinks he can tame.

Well, I got news for him—the last man who tried to tame me didn't walk away unscathed. None of them ever do.

"I don't expect any of that," he insists.

"Really?" I challenge, my gaze narrowing.

Slowly, he lowers his arms, and leaning just a fraction closer, murmurs, "Not saying I'd turn you down if you were naked and begging."

A shock of lust runs through me, like a zap of electric current. It pebbles my nipples and sends a flush of heat up my chest. I'm sure I'm starting to look like a tomato, but denial still seems like the best course of action.

"That's not going to happen."

"If you say so, darlin'." He leans back and mirrors my posture by crossing his thick arms over his enticingly wide chest.

"I've never begged a man for anything in all my life, and I don't plan on starting with you."

"No problem." He shrugs like it's no big deal, making my blood boil. "And the same goes for you."

"What?"

"No falling in love with me, either."

"Not a chance in hell of that happening."

His eyes darken, and the corner of his mouth twitches upward as if enjoying this back and forth. "Just think...we don't even need to stay married. Once we have our business launched—maybe with an event to make it official—and once I'm in the controlling seat at Canyon Spring Ranch, we can call it done. Divorce, annulment, whatever. Once we both get what we're after, we can go our separate ways."

"A gala would be perfect. But what about the business?" I test, still not sure I trust his intentions. "We'll be partners, after all. We can't just walk away from that."

"Not from the green partnership, no. But from each other... why not? Like you said, it's a business agreement, nothing more."

"Absolutely nothing more," I echo, my jaw aching from the clench of my teeth.

He dips his head in agreement.

"Okay, then. It's a deal."

"Well, all right," he drawls. "Should we shake on it?"

I must be out of my damn mind.

Am I really so desperate that I'd say *I do* to a man whose family is the bane of my father's existence? Or to any man for that matter? Surely, I could make a deal with his brother Ridge that doesn't involve nuptials.

But the look on Brooks's face—his stupidly handsome face—tells me he really is my only hope. Ridge would do exactly as described—steal my ideas, crush my hopes, and leave me to flounder with a knife in my back.

If there's one thing I want less than marriage, it's giving up control of my ranch and my dream, especially if it means being stepped on in the process. So that puts going to Ridge out of the question.

I fill my lungs, steel my spine, and place the palm of my trembling hand in Brooks's, sealing our deal the old-fashioned way.

Yep, I really am this desperate. Or just plain old crazy.

His smile pulls higher at one side, a dimple forming between laugh lines. "Sit and have a drink with me." His breath coasts across my skin, causing goosebumps to rise everywhere. *Everywhere.*

God, why does he keep touching me?

Why do I keep letting him?

I could melt into a puddle right now I'm so turned on. Then he wouldn't need a drink, he could just lap me up off the floor.

Now there's an ill-timed and highly inappropriate thought. Although, it might have some merit.

"Do you think another drink's really a good idea?" I scold, snapping to my senses, although he isn't acting all that drunk.

"Why not?" His brows draw together, and he takes a step back, his hands falling away from me in the process.

Good. His proximity is only confusing things, and I need

all my wits about me if I'm going to come out of this new deal on top.

Or on the bottom.

Despite my insistence otherwise, I really wouldn't mind being under him.

"Addie." His tone has an air of audacious authority. Like he's got me right where he wants me.

Handsome jackass.

"No. I'm not interested in continuing this conversation until you're sober and our deal's in writing. Right now, I can't trust what you're saying isn't all due to alcohol and whatever this is all about." I wave my hand around his bruised face.

"I told you; I'm not drunk. Come on...you won't even join me for one drink to celebrate?"

"How about we save the celebration for when both our ranches are running on green energy and every part of the plan is fulfilled?" I smirk, gaining the upper hand. "Besides, you already drank my beer."

His head turns, his eyes finally moving away from me to the table and the array of empty glasses, including my recently emptied beer mug.

Not missing the opportunity, I rush toward the door, calling back over my shoulder, "Call me when you're sober."

Thankfully, he doesn't try to stop me this time. I'm not sure I could resist him if he did. All the fight's seeped out of me, zapped away by my body's annoying, out of place urges. Urges I need to get good and under control.

I might end up married to Brooks Kincaide, but no way in hell am I sleeping with him.

In my rush to flee, I stumble out the tavern door and nearly fall face-first into my recent ex-fling, Derek. Go figure.

This town's too small for us not to run into each other, but I'd hoped to avoid him for just a little longer. I certainly hadn't planned on smacking right into him with my head in the clouds and hormones running amok.

In the process of trying to dodge physical contact, I step awkwardly to the side, twisting my ankle, and a distressed cry rushes past my tight lips.

"Addison." His mouth drops open and body goes rigid, but he makes no move to help me.

He simply stares as I hop around, muttering curses under my breath. "Fuck, fuck, fuckity-fuck." Well...some of those might not have been as quiet as intended.

"What are you doing here?" he asks, oblivious to my pain.

"Me?" I finally settle in one place, keeping my weight on my non-throbbing ankle. "Why, I'm just learning a new dance. What the hell does it look like?"

My feet become his new fascination, and he rubs the back of his neck. "You're still mad at me?"

"Mad at you?" What is going on today? Have the men in this town finally ganged up to mess with me?

"Yeah, you know..." His eyes dart up to mine, hesitant and unsure. "For asking you to marry me?"

Shit. I never should've left the ranch.

"I'm not mad at you, Derek. I'm just not ready—" The words lodge in my throat. *Not ready for marriage.*

It's what I'd told him right before I broke it off. Right before he accused me of being a cold, unfeeling, heartbreaking bitch.

I don't think I'm any of those things, and in my defense, I had no idea he was anywhere close to a proposal. We only dated a few months, and most of those dates consisted of stilted conversation over dinner, followed by drinks, then sex.

The sex was okay, but hardly worth the effort of getting there.

Truthfully, even if Derek hadn't blown up our relationship with his horrifying and painfully out of place proposal, I'd planned to end things, anyway.

He isn't a terrible guy, but he's definitely not the guy for me.

The door of the tavern creaks behind me, and I realize I'm still standing in front of it, blocking anyone else from leaving. But when I try to move out of the way, my twisted ankle screams in protest.

"Shit!" I yelp, teetering precariously on one foot.

A strong arm wraps around my waist, securing me, and I'm pulled back against a wall of solid man.

"I got ya, darlin'," Brooks's voice rumbles in my ear. "You okay?"

Am I okay? Well, let's see. I'm in the arms of a man who, because of a family feud, I'm supposed to hate but to whom I'm now betrothed, while my ex, whose marriage proposal I crushed along with his heart, is staring daggers at us. And oh, my ankle might be sprained. But sure, I'm just fucking peachy.

"I'm fine," I grumble, trying to extricate myself from his hold.

But the stubborn jackass won't let me go.

"What's this all about?" Derek demands, his eyes brewing

with something that looks like wounded male pride and possible murder.

"It's nothing," I say, hoping he's planning where to bury Brooks's body and not mine.

But at the same time, Brooks growls, "None of your business."

"If it involves Addison, then it is my business." Derek's tone sends a slow crawl up my spine. "She's my girlfriend."

What the actual hell?

"Is she now?" Brooks's voice is low and even—no hint of what he might be thinking or planning to do.

I place my hand over his, hoping he gets the message to just let this thing go.

But men can be such slow, senseless, stubborn creatures.

"*Addison*?" Brooks says my name like a dare. "You didn't mention you were in a relationship."

If I wasn't in so much pain, I'd unleash my fists on him. I think it'd feel rather satisfying to add to his collection of scrapes and bruises.

"Brooks," I snarl, turning in his arms and placing both hands on his chest, my eyes broadcasting my desire for him to shut the hell up. "I believe I promised you a ride home."

He returns my gaze with a knowing smirk.

Jackass.

"Derek," I call as I hobble away, ushering Brooks toward my truck. "I'm sorry you didn't get the memo, but you and I are done. If you need me to explain it again, you'll have to call me later."

Harsh? Maybe. But I thought I'd made it clear when I

broke it off with him, and something tells me he's still not getting the message.

I climb into my truck where Brooks is already belted into the passenger seat and hightail it away from my ex as fast as possible without breaking the law or running anyone over.

"That was fun," Brooks says through a drunk sounding chuckle. "Not awkward at all."

"No, not at all." I steal a glance his way, a smile teasing the corner of my lips. "Told you not to go falling in love with me, didn't I?"

Our eyes meet, and we both burst out laughing.

5

BROOKS

I stumble into the dining room, eager for a jolt of caffeine, and while nearly all of us still live at home, on the ranch, Laken's the only one still having breakfast. She eyes me warily from across the table as if I'm a two-headed horse and I pour a cup of black coffee.

"Just say what you have to say before you fry your brain thinkin' on it too hard." The first gulp of the steaming brew is a welcomed burn down my throat.

"What?" She nearly spews her coffee when straightening her spine like she has a stick up her ass.

"You're giving me the side-eye. Just say whatever's going on in that head of yours." I shove a strip of crispy bacon into my mouth and lick my fingers for good measure.

The fork tines break the perfectly round, vibrant yolk of the fried egg on my plate. It looks a lot like the yellowy orange fireball of a Montana sunset.

"Are you okay?" She pushes a stray blonde lock into her ponytail, and I'm taken aback.

My youngest sister isn't shy, and with twelve years between us, we aren't close, so I'm unsure what to make of her question. She's concerned for me? I shove half the egg in my mouth and study her.

Laken usually steers clear of me. If she ever needs a man's opinion or support—most times she does just fine on her own—Pa was her first choice and Ridge a close second. I've never made the cut and don't know why that is.

"I mean, you don't look so good." Her finger toys with the rim of her cup, gaze glued to the table. "I suppose it's to be expected. You had everything you've ever worked for snatched out from under you."

I suck air between my teeth, not willing to listen to this bullshit.

"Missy, it ain't over until it's over." My chair scrapes across the wooden floor, causing her to flinch, as I get to my feet. "I know which horse you're backing, but don't count your winnings just yet."

My linen napkin slaps against the table, and I take one final swig of coffee to wash down the rest of the egg that suddenly tastes of sawdust. The fine china clatters when I drop it onto the saucer. Without another look, I march from the room and to the back of the house where we have the ranch offices.

"Brooks, I didn't mean it like that," she calls after me. Her regret does nothing to pierce through my fiery determination.

The head seat of Canyon Spring Ranch is mine, and I'm getting it back, starting now.

To be expected, Mama's in Pa's office, standing behind his desk, culling through papers when I barge in. The door smacks against the wall, and her head snaps up.

"Brooks." She glowers and my name comes out like a curse.

Her surprise doesn't last long though, and she quickly remembers who she is, or more likely who she thinks I am. She couldn't be more wrong.

"You can't come bustin' in like that. I've had enough of your outbursts." She cocks a hip and places a hand on her jeans-clad waist. "You were an utter disgrace outside of Butler's yesterday. All of Prospect had a bird's-eye view to you throwing down with your brother like you did."

She rounds the desk, eyes still narrowed into shards of icy blue. "Not to mention you going to Ruby's."

I roll my eyes, not in the least bit surprised she's aware of my visit to the local watering hole. She didn't hear it from Cole—he's definitely still balls deep in the redhead.

But her sources aren't necessarily in the family. People in this town will give up long buried secrets just for cheap thrills. Heck, Ruby could be the one who blabbed about my business.

Does Mama already know about Addie? Does she have any idea we cooked up a scheme right under half the town's noses?

"I understand yesterday was difficult." She pulls at the hem of her blouse as if it's bunched or wrinkled—it isn't— before her shrewd gaze snags mine. "It was hard for all of us.

And I'll overlook your behavior, drowning your sorrows like that, so unbecoming of a Kincaide. Brooks, pull yourself together. This is why things are the way they are."

Her final words are vague and mild, but it's a punch in the throat. My mouth is cotton dry, air lodging in my lungs, and fury burns at the base of my spine.

She's referring to the will, justifying why my father thought it best to overlook his firstborn to run the ranch in favor of his second son. There's no excuse when I've given my life to this family, proven myself every step of the way. I'm no longer sitting back and letting shit happen.

"Pa was a smart man." A hoarse rumble erupts from deep within me, and I lean into her, so close I can see the flecks of golden green and navy in her blue irises. "But he was wrong about Ridge running the ranch."

"Well, it was his choice." Her answer is pat and only serves to fuel my fire.

"Obviously, he wasn't completely convinced Ridge was the *one*."

"Whatever are you talking about?" She inches backward, her thighs hitting the edge of the desk.

Nowhere else to go, Mama.

"If he was dead set on Ridge, why not just give it to him?" I arch a brow and she opens her mouth, but I rush on. "But no. He had stipulations, things we both know Ridge isn't going to readily give up. His bachelor life? Not going to happen."

My brother doesn't run around, but he's also never had a serious relationship. I've often wondered if he'll ever settle down. And I think Pa wondered, too.

"You don't know that. Ridge will do what's required of him."

"He won't meet the terms of the will. Besides, you're the one who makes the final decision."

She's still, holding her tongue, but her gaze sharpens, and I could be wishing on a penny in a well, but her silence is something akin to agreement.

"Ridge wants to run the ranch." She's haughty in her assessment, like that says it all.

"I'm sure he does, but I want it more. And I'm the better choice. When he was off at college out of state, who was here, going to college close to home to keep helping out? Who has been here every time something needed to be done? Me."

My fingers jab at my chest, and I'm reminded of the cold stabbing sensation when Ridge was named head of the ranch —my dream.

"I will meet the terms of the will. Already ahead of him. I'm getting married Saturday."

Her eyes widen, and for the second time, she's rendered speechless.

"Before you ask, it's Addison Monroe. We're both coming at this as a business partnership in more ways than one. In addition to getting married, we're also embarking on a sustainability plan for both our ranches."

"Married? Addie Monroe? A sustainability plan?"

Is there an echo in here? She's dumbfounded, but not in a bad way. Dare I say, Sage Kincaide looks impressed.

I stand to my full six feet two and try not to be too smug, crossing my arms over my chest.

"Mama, I was thinking—" Ridge stands in the doorway,

eyes flitting from our mother to me and back again warily. "Am I interrupting?"

"No, come on in." I wave my hand for him to join us, beaming from ear to ear and all too happy to set my brother straight. "I'm glad you're here. I've got some news, and you might as well hear it now."

He's tentative, shuffling in, as if sensing he shouldn't be too sure he wants to know what's going on.

"I'm getting married to Addison Monroe. You'll be getting your invitation tomorrow."

He jolts as if electrocuted, jaw hanging open, and I barrel on with my one-two punch since things could stall here if they decide to challenge me on our future plans.

"And we're rolling out a plan to green both our ranches. We're going to make the launch public to the town with a gala where we'll talk about the opportunities for local businesses, the benefits and tax credits, and how, once we're up and running, we'll have the infrastructure in place to assist others who want to do the same. Other ranches will want to join."

Ridge barks out a laugh, slapping his hand against his thigh, but he quickly curbs his amusement when neither of us respond in kind. Mama raises her brow and tightens her lips, causing tiny wrinkles to spring to the corners of her mouth.

"You're not joking, are you?" He wipes an eye and composes himself.

"Not one bit." I clench my jaw and stare intently. "I'll take you through the details of the plan soon. But for now, just know it'll be profitable, and the Kincaides and Monroes will be leading the way for Prospect."

"Shit, Brooks, I-I...that's a lot to unpack." He stares at our mother, who's keenly interested and unusually quiet.

"A sustainability plan is long overdue. I was meaning to talk to Pa about it. But why do we need the Monroes?" He rubs at his jaw, fixing me with a determined gaze. "We'll do it on our own. We don't need Addison Monroe."

And so it begins. Like I thought, there'd be no partnership if Ridge took the lead. It will always be his way or the highway.

"Addison will be my wife, and we're in this together. I don't have time to go over it all right now, but when I do, Addie will be here."

In two quick strides, I'm at the door where I halt, feeling their unspoken and surely snide comments poking at my back. Then it hits me. I shouldn't be surprised or disappointed—why would I expect or hope for more?

This is my life. Always has been.

Before leaving the two vultures to pick me apart, I glance over my shoulder. "And thank you."

Their equally puzzled expressions fetch a smile from me and loosen the tension in my chest.

"Thank you for what?" Ridge asks.

"For congratulating me on getting married."

Like earlier with Laken, I ignore their contrite calls and stroll through the offices of the Canyon Spring Ranch, feeling that much closer to what I most want.

ddie jumps from her truck, long golden waves bouncing down her back, as I drive up to her home. She pauses in opening the back passenger door and watches my every step toward her.

"Good afternoon, darlin'." My smile is wide and sincere.

"Not that again. Please don't call me darlin'." She tries for sugary sweet, but it's forced and dry.

"But it suits you, and pretty soon, that's exactly what you'll be."

Turning to face me, she places her hands on her hips. "I've got work to do. Can I help you with something?"

With the truck door open, she turns and leans into the back, reaching for a box resting on the backseat bench.

"I came to tell my bride-to-be that the wedding's Saturday."

"Saturday?" She releases the box and faces me again.

"You heard me." I nod, gifting her a lopsided grin.

"I can't possibly—"

"Don't get ahead of yourself and start worrying. You've only got one thing you need to do for Saturday. Well, make that two." I hold up two fingers, and she rolls her eyes.

"What's that?" She lifts a delicate hand to shield her eyes from the bright afternoon sun.

"Be there." My smile widens at her unimpressed expression. "I've got everything under control."

She opens and closes her mouth a few times before finally asking, "You do?" Disbelief laces her words, and I chuckle, nodding.

Addison Monroe at a loss for words is going to take some

getting used to. And while I'm a fan of her smart mouth, her speechless side is mighty attractive in a challenging kind of way.

Her eyes flicker with a wide-eyed frustration, waiting for my response. No, that's not the right word. It's more like... passion. Yeah, that's it.

I'm starting to see she's passionate about most things, even those that most people would let slide. She loves a challenge and doesn't scare easily. I mean, she approached me about the greening plan, risking ridicule and me possibly calling her crazy.

Tapping her foot, she clears her throat. "And what's the second thing you said I had to do?"

"If you haven't already, tell your daddy about our upcoming nuptials."

She's quick to hide it, but for a split second, she blanches. Telling George Monroe his only daughter's marrying the son of his mortal enemy isn't going to be easy. But if anyone can do it, Addie can.

"You worry about telling your family, and I'll do the same with mine." She pats at my chest, and it takes everything in me not to grab her hand and keep it there, near my now racing heart.

"Already have." I'm a cocky bastard, and again, she hides her surprise well but I'm on to her.

"And about you having everything under control, what makes you think I want a man handling all the details?" She lifts her chin and sniffs, not amused with my attempt at chivalry. "It's my wedding, after all."

"True, but darlin', I want to save you the headache and

worry. Besides, why go to the trouble of all that stress when it's for show anyway. We both know you don't care."

She opens her mouth to say something but snaps it tight just as quickly, studying me. With a long inhale, she stands her ground. "I want a say. Always."

"Really? Duly noted." I scratch at the scruff on my jaw and dip my chin. "Just be there, looking pretty, and all will be fine."

"Don't treat me like cattle to be branded. I'm not your property. I'll tell you right now, Brooks Kincaide, I'm your equal or nothing else in this marriage." She waggles her finger at me, her cheeks pinkening to a lovely shade of rose.

I bite back my smile. Something tells me she'd be sure to wipe it off my face before I can spell my name.

"I wouldn't have it any other way, little darlin'." I wink and tip the brim of my Stetson.

Her nostrils flare and soft, cherry lips twist, but there's fire in her eyes that I can't say I don't like. In fact, it damn near turns me on.

Addie may act like she doesn't like this, whatever this is between us—the fervent push and pull—but her delight burns bright in the flame of her gaze.

She likes my teasing.

Oh, this is going to be fun.

6

ADDISON

*B*rooks Kincaide might be the most infuriating man I've ever met.

No, there's no question, he most definitely *is*.

After giving me no choice in the arrangement of our wedding—insisting he had it covered—he now has the nerve to be late to the ceremony.

Aggravating jackass.

Normally, I'd balk at being told what to do by a man who thinks he knows better than me. Last week, for example, I almost socked Jimmy Smith in the jaw for arguing about which fertilizer I should buy, like I haven't done my research and know which brand is best for the environment. If it weren't for Sheriff Gilbert strolling in at that exact moment, Jimmy would be sporting a busted lip.

I like Jimmy, but it's the principle of the thing.

Yet, this time with Brooks, I let it go. I let him take over and dictate the details of the wedding because I figure there's no point in starting a war with the man who's helping to secure my future. At least not over this—anything to do with my ranch or the greening project and he'll be in a world of hurt.

Besides, this isn't a real marriage. Why should it bother me that we're not having a real wedding?

It's not like I have a scrapbook of fancy wedding dreams buried in a box at the bottom of my closet. Or like I dug it out last night and memorialized the pages over a tub of Chunky Monkey and a stream of tears.

And so what if I did?

I'm allowed to mourn the wasted dreams of my youth. Even if I gave up on them long ago.

"Nervous?" my best friend, Hannah, asks, reaching up to fix a rogue strand of my pinned hair.

She's gorgeous—all-natural in a flowing lavender dress and heels that bring her five-foot-nothin' frame up to my chin. Her red hair is piled into a messy bun, adding to the illusion of height, and the wedding ring on her finger competes with her smile for attention.

Next to her, in a borrowed white eyelet dress and nude flats, I feel like a fraud.

"The ceremony was supposed to start five minutes ago," I hiss, looking to the clock on the wall for the hundredth time. "Where is he?"

Why isn't he here?

"He'll be here," she reassures me, glancing across the sterile room of the Helena courthouse to her husband, Parker, who's standing with my dad.

Both men are watching us, Parker beaming his Hollywood-bright smile and Daddy glowering like he's about to witness a funeral instead of a wedding. Although, in his mind, they might be one and the same.

I shift from foot to foot and try to tune out the loud ticking of the clock.

"Relax," Hannah urges. "This was his idea, remember?"

"Yes, but maybe he's having second thoughts." Not that I'd blame him. I spent a solid three hours this morning talking myself into, then out of, and back into this half-baked plan of ours.

"That's the nerves talking." She smirks. "Remember what a mess I was before my wedding?"

Is it only nerves? I shake out my arms, my fingers feeling tingly and my whole body full of jitters.

"You were deliriously in love."

"Sure, but I still worried I was making a mistake by marrying a celebrity and upending everything stable about my life."

"Oh, God," I groan, my empty stomach churning. "You think I'm making a mistake, don't you?"

Daddy grunts with displeasure, vocalizing his opinion on the subject. Again. But at least he's here and, despite his aversion, he hasn't disowned me yet.

"You've made bigger." Hannah smiles.

Dammit, this must be a mistake, otherwise he'd be here. Wouldn't he?

"Name one." I'm desperate for a distraction—anything that'll take my mind off all the horrible ways this could go wrong.

But before she has a chance to reply, the door bursts open and Brooks stalks in.

He's clean shaven and dressed in a suit, but his hair is a sexy mess, like he's just rolled out of bed or has been combing his fingers through it, repeatedly.

When he looks up, our gazes collide, and his brisk steps falter and slow. The fierce, determined set of his jaw softens, as does the bite of his blue gaze.

Still, he reaches me in only a few short strides. "Wow, Addie," he breathes, his voice deep and rough. "You look..."

"You're late," I snap, refusing to fall prey to his compliments.

Pretty words mean nothing, and I've heard them all before. What I need is action. A partner who'll take a stand and show me he means the things he says. A partner who's true and won't let me down. A man who's on-freaking-time to his own damn wedding.

"I'm sorry." His eyes search mine and he grasps me by the elbow. "I tried—"

His words are cut short when the door opens again and members of his family cascade through.

Sage Kincaide, recent widow of the infamous Devlin and my soon-to-be mother-in-law, glides up the center aisle as though on a Paris runway. She's flawless—perfect skin, perfect hair, stunning dress. And one hundred percent stone cold.

Her late husband may have been the one with the feared reputation, but something tells me this woman's wrath would be a million times worse. Just the look in her ice-blue eyes makes me squirm.

She's flanked by Brooks's siblings Trey, Ridge, and Scarlett, each looking closed-off and doubtful. Cole saunters behind them all, like he's just here for the show and hopefully a good time later.

"Well, this is...quaint," Scarlett announces, her mouth twisting to a phony smile as she scans the white walls and empty seats.

Leave it to Scarlett Kincaide to find fault in a moment that has nothing to do with her.

I may not know her well—or at all, really—but she reminds me of every school-yard bully and bitchy drama-queen I grew up with. None of those girls liked me much then—when I was a gangly teenage tomboy—and I still don't like any of them to this day.

Scarlett may not have been one of them, but I don't think I like her much, all the same.

"Yes," Sage drawls, her eyes glued on me. "Quaint, indeed."

My hackles rise, and I bite my tongue to stop myself from saying something I'll regret later.

Beside me, Brooks's demeanor has shifted. His hold on me tightens, and I can feel his body tense as he leans closer. "I really am sorry," he whispers, his warm breath trailing down the column of my neck.

I shiver. Whether it's from the contact or the calculating stare of his mother, I can't be sure, but I'm given no further time to ponder.

The officiant enters the room, brushing back his mop of hair. "Are we all present?"

"Yes, sir." Brooks takes a step away from me, folding his hands to fists at his sides.

My legs feel like rubber bands about to snap, but I somehow quell my urge to run and stand at stiff attention beside him.

This is it. No backing down now.

There's some shuffling behind me as our guests take their seats and the officiant begins the ceremony.

It's short and simple—a standard contract, with some bits about devotion and honor thrown in but the mention of love noticeably missing—and I convince myself it's for the best.

Brooks and I may not be marrying for traditional reasons, but that doesn't make it wrong. In fact, I'd say our bargain is the best reason of all. Two people with mutual interests and no messy emotions to screw it up.

If one of us chooses to walk away, no one will get hurt.

When the officiant instructs us to face each other, our gazes collide yet again. My anger with him dissipates, replaced with a spark of something magnetic. It passes between us, the feeling of an electric current, pulling us closer together.

Brooks takes my hand, and I swallow back my fear and doubt as we exchange rings with our eyes locked on one another.

"I now pronounce you husband and wife," the officiant confirms. "You may kiss."

Brooks's mouth descends on mine in a rush, and I'm overcome by a wave of unexpected sensation. His lips are warm, inviting, and press to mine in a way that promises greater things to come.

But as quickly as it began, it's over. He draws back, his eyes catching mine one last time, before dropping his hold on me and turning away.

"Thank you." He shakes the officiant's hand.

Cole slaps him on the back, beaming, and Brooks turns to hug him, leaving me to wonder what the hell just happened and what comes next.

"See," Hannah murmurs, "nothing to worry about."

I turn to her and am engulfed in her arms. For such a tiny thing, she sure knows how to give a big dose of comfort.

When I look up from her embrace, I find Daddy standing close. His mouth is still drawn down in a hard scowl, but there's no mistaking the warmth in his eyes.

He loves me. Even if I am a terrible disappointment.

"Daddy." My voice breaks, and I take a step toward him. "Daddy, I—"

"All right, everyone!" Sage's no-nonsense tone cuts through the moment, disrupting conversations and slicing a frigid path along my heart. "I'm taking you all to Walter's North Bistro. There's a dress code, but I've already secured a table."

"That's not necessary." Brooks's tone is polite, but I can see the muscle at his jaw ticking. "Ruby's expecting us at her place."

Sage's detached demeanor falters for just a moment, a look of hurt flashing across her features. "Nonsense," she says, the coolness seeping back firmly into place.

"I'm fine with Ruby's," I assert, sensing Brooks's discomfort.

Sage turns her venomous gaze my way. "You're a Kincaide

now, dear Addison, and Kincaides do not celebrate special occasions at the local dive."

"Please don't speak to her that way." Brooks's hand slides into mine, the move feeling both protective and overbearing at the same time.

"I'm outta here," Ridge grumbles. He places his hat on his head and tips it toward me, mumbling, "Congratulations," before heading for the door.

"I should go, too," Daddy agrees, but stands rooted in place. "Can't leave Hank in charge all day."

"Fine," Sage huffs. "Do what you want. But Brooks, I expect you at your rightful place, performing your duty to your family tomorrow. No excuses."

Speechless, I watch her link arms with Scarlett and Trey and casually strut away.

"What the hell?" I turn to Brooks, blood pumping hard through my veins.

But he refuses to look my way, his gaze stuck on his family who've all but abandoned him on his wedding day—and all because Sage didn't get her way.

All, that is, except Cole, who's standing to the side with his phone in hand. I can't tell if he's indifferent or just trying to stay out of the way.

"Brooks?" I urge, tugging on his hand.

He clears his throat, releases me, and turns to our remaining guests with a bright, lopsided smile. "Who's up for a few drinks?"

The alcohol's flowing through me, warming me up and helping me forget why I needed so many drinks in the first place.

It's a nice change of pace.

"Feel better?" Hannah wraps her arms around me.

"Much." I lean into her embrace, but my attention remains glued to the dance floor where Brooks is keeping time with the music, two-stepping along with the crowd.

We never made it to Ruby's. Heck, we didn't make it out of Helena.

Brooks suggested we stay in the city to celebrate the start of our partnership. I'd been hesitant, not wanting to upset Daddy further, but Hannah urged me to give him space and to take some time out to relax.

"You were right," I admit, squeezing her tight. "I needed a night of fun like this."

"Darn straight, girl." She pulls back from our hug, her eyes sparkling. "Now maybe go have some more fun with the hunk of a man you just married. And by fun, I mean the naked sweaty kind."

Just the thought makes me giddy, and I laugh, shaking my head. "He is tempting, isn't he? But I can't."

"Heck, yes...I mean, why not?"

I sling back the rest of my drink, not exactly avoiding her question but hoping to maybe find a bit of resolve.

"It's not part of our deal," I finally answer, the alcohol warming my belly. "I don't want to complicate this thing with feelings."

"Who said anything about feelings?" She nudges me,

directing my attention back to the man in question and his ridiculously enticing body.

I've always been a sucker for a man who can dance.

Parker staggers toward us, winded from his failed attempt to keep up with the group. Poor guy looks close to collapse. "Ready to go?" he calls.

"You're leaving?" I pout and hug Hannah one more time.

"Don't worry," she says in my ear. "I think you'll be in very capable hands."

Just as I step back from her, the hands in question wrap around my waist. "Come dance with me," Brooks growls in my ear, tugging me toward the dance floor.

"Have fun!" Hannah waves goodbye with a huge grin.

"Where's Cole?" I shout over the music, linking my hand with his as we fall into pace with the rest of the crowd.

"I think he left with the blonde, or maybe the brunette. Hell, knowing him, he's probably gone upstairs with them both."

I laugh, and he swings me around the dance floor, his enthusiasm contagious.

We stomp our feet, hooting and hollering through three upbeat songs before the music slows. A twangy country ballad pumps through the speakers, and the atmosphere of the swanky hotel bar suddenly takes on an intimate quality.

I wobble, the liquor making me unsteady on my feet, but Brooks helps balance me, pulling me close as we begin swaying to the music.

"This has been a really great night," I murmur, setting my head on his shoulder.

He hums his agreement. "It has, but it's not over yet."

The strangers around us seem to fade into the background as my focus zeroes in on the electric sensation of his hands on my body.

Damn, it feels good to be in his arms this way. Like it's just the two of us.

Husband and wife.

My blood pumps harder as his fingers trail up my spine and tangle in my hair. I savor the feel of his sturdy back under my palms, the steady, almost graceful rocking of his body against mine, and the way the unmistakable ridge of his hardening cock teases me just above the apex of my thighs.

"Let's get a room," I pant, allowing my hands to roam the solid wall of his chest.

"Already got one." His hand covers mine, and he dips me slowly, bending until there's nothing holding me from the ground but him.

I groan as he sets me upright, our bodies pressed tight in all the right places.

"Come on, darlin'." He pulls me by the hand, away from the dancing couples and slow beat of the music, through the open doorway of the bar, across the hotel lobby, and into a waiting elevator.

Still holding tight to my hand, he pushes the button for the fourth floor, and the doors slide closed.

"When did you get a room?"

He turns to me and cups the side of my face in his big, rough hand. "Is that really what you want to talk about right now?"

"No," I admit. "I don't want to talk at all."

His mouth quirks as though humored, but his gaze smolders with desire. Slowly—ever so freaking slowly—he lowers his lips to mine, stealing my breath in a passionate kiss.

The elevator stops, the doors whoosh open, and we stumble down the hall together, still attached at the mouth.

Brooks fumbles with the key card, not moving his lips from mine, and somehow opens the door. We rush into the room in a tangle of arms and legs, and then things really heat up.

Pushing me against the closed door, he drags his mouth down my neck, showering me with kisses and setting me on fire with the hot glide of his tongue against my skin.

"You look fucking gorgeous today, Addie," he says between kisses, his hands sliding over my breasts.

Incoherently, I moan and try to tug him closer.

"I wanted to say it sooner. Wanted to tell you how hard you made me, but..." His words trail off. But not because he's kissing me.

I crack open my eyes, looking up to his stupidly handsome face, and see him wearing a dark frown. "But I was a bitch," I finish for him.

"What?"

"It's okay." I push away from the door and squeeze past him. "I guess I have that reputation for a reason."

"No, Addie." His arm shoots out to stop me. "I don't think that. You're not."

We're close, and even though we were much, much closer only a moment ago, it's suddenly more than I can handle.

This was not supposed to happen. This relationship is fake.

Fake. Fake. Fake.

And I'm breaking my own damn rules.

"Brooks, I'm too drunk for this." It's a lie, and he probably knows it, but it's the only defense I've got. "I hope you got a room with double beds."

7

BROOKS

Spears of marigold shower the bed, the sun warm and bright, and my eyes slowly open, blinking a few times as I get my bearings. A hint of lavender violet wafts through the air, compelling the corners of my mouth to kick up into a gratified smile.

Yesterday comes back to me, and the pad of one finger rubs at the gold band firmly encircling my ring finger.

Our wedding.

Addison Monroe...well, no, Addison Monroe-Kincaide is now my wife.

I roll over in bed to greet the missus, a smile still painting my face until I find the other side empty. I sit up and throw off the covers, wearing only boxers, and pad across the lush carpet toward the slightly open bathroom door.

"Addie?" There's no sound coming from the other side, and with two fingers, I gently push the door wide open. "Addie?"

No one is here, and from the looks of it, nothing in the bathroom has been touched. What on earth? Did she even stay here last night?

Making a beeline for the bed, I flatten my hand onto the pillow where she should have slept, and it's cool to the touch. She's been gone a while. And why the hell didn't I hear her leave?

There's only one place Addie would go, and if she thinks she can run and hide, she's sorely mistaken. It's time to go to her ranch.

It's barely past six in the morning, and barring a bender the night before, I'm cursed with years of rising with the sun, which suits me just fine about now. There's plenty of time to shower, check out of the hotel, and get to her home before she's off doing whatever it is she does.

Our marriage may only be on paper, but this is no way to start things. Our first morning as husband and wife and I'm already behind the eight ball, wrestling to tie her down. Addie would scowl if she could hear my ramblings.

I snicker, dropping my boxers and hopping into the hot water cascading from the huge chrome faucet above. This marble shower is big enough to fit two comfortably.

Addie.

To think, we could have put this shower to good use.

Who am I kidding?

Last night was...something else. I thought I'd blown the whole deal when I showed up late to the courthouse. It took everything short of a miracle to get my mother and some of the family to the wedding.

In hindsight, I shouldn't have even bothered to invite

them, but selfishly, I couldn't resist rubbing it in Mama and Ridge's faces. Neither believed I'd go through with the wedding.

And now, I'm one step closer to taking what's mine. Canyon Spring Ranch.

When I barged through the doors of that dreary room, my family reluctantly in tow, and caught sight of Addie waiting for me, I had an overwhelming desire to do something drastic.

The mixture of worry and anger on her face made me want to whisk her away. Save for her friends, the sour faces in that room brought out my protective streak and an intense desire to make the wedding about the two of us.

Forget the deal, or shelve the deal for a few hours, at any rate. The ceremony didn't need to be depressing and painful.

Foolish, yeah, but it was hard not to want more with Addie wearing that simple yet beautiful white dress. Her blonde hair shimmering. She looked eager, vulnerable, and raw...it had almost felt real.

I wanted her something fierce, and as the night wore on, holding her in my arms, chest to chest on the dance floor, the want only deepened and intensified. It damn near killed me to back off when she put a stop to things in the hotel room, seconds away from consummating the marriage.

Sex wasn't part of the deal, but she'd been so willing. Hungry eyes, roaming hands, needy mouth. Damn, that mouth of hers and her taste. Sweet as honey with a hint of something tart like huckleberries, and even still, I could taste her fiery spirit.

The pull of attraction was frenetic and as unstoppable as

a heart attack. Just thinking about it now brings an ache to my chest...and to my balls.

I turn the shower dial, cooling the water fast and with it, hopefully, my raging desire. I can't hunt down my wife with my cock as hard as steel and need as savage as a beast.

One freezing shower and a ride back to Prospect cools me down enough to face Addie. Emerging onto her front porch, she doesn't so much as greet me but sweeps a disinterested gaze from my head to my toes, then wordlessly, she spins on her heel and walks back into the house.

I follow her to the dining room where a simple collection of foods and coffee are on a large table set for two.

"Aw, you shouldn't have." I plunk myself in front of an empty plate and pour a coffee.

Her eyes widen, and a hand flies to the curve of her hip. "That's Daddy's seat. Get out."

"Well, darlin', that isn't any way to treat your husband. I've got a long, hard day ahead of me, and a man's gotta eat." I pick up the knife and fork, frowning at the slim pickings. "No eggs or bacon?"

"Brooks, get up." Her lips are a thin line, and the muscle in her jaw bounces. "Please."

"I tell you what." I lean forward, elbows on the table, staring up at her. "I'll sit at another spot, closer to you—" My knife points at the empty chair beside where I'm guessing she usually sits. "—if you explain to me why you thought it was a good idea to hightail it out of our bed without so much as a goodbye to your *husband*."

The emphasis on my final word causes her to flinch. Her

brows knit as she studies me, and I can almost hear the thoughts galloping through her head.

I'm only now getting to know Addison, but we've been together enough in this short period of time that I figure she's weighing her options.

She's feisty and bold, so some of her choices will be severe and sure to prove her point while others will be tamer and, I'd say, more mature. But her concern with the latter would be that I don't understand or take her seriously.

A sly, lopsided grin skates across my mouth and her own mouth tightens. I'm enjoying this, and I can tell my amused reaction, like a match to firewood, sets her ire ablaze.

"I always start my day with Daddy." She's stern, but something pokes at my chest. The way her eyes warm and mouth softens at the mention of her father.

The loyalty and love she has for him is foreign to me, or more the unwavering want to start her day with the same person, every day, no matter what.

Sure, my family gathers daily for breakfast, but we're passing ships, each of us in and out, grabbing food and on our way. It's more about the food—the need for sustenance —than anything to do with the company.

"Well, I'm your husband now." Her devotion pisses me off, and my tone sharpens. "And it's time to start new traditions."

"Our marriage doesn't change things. Not something as important as this. My father, this house, and the ranch are my home. And Brooks—" She's closer now, hovering, and her subtle fragrance plays with my senses, causing me to push back in the chair. "—our marriage doesn't change that."

"Well, that's where you're wrong, darlin'. We're a couple now, our lives are entwined whether you like it or not, and I can't have you living here and me at Canyon Spring Ranch. We need to be together."

"Well, that's simple. You live here with me." She's smug, straightening to her full height, and I'm about to give her a piece of my mind when her father ambles into the room, walking a little slower than usual.

The Monroe patriarch clears his throat, narrowing his unwelcoming gaze on me and I'm unfazed, fully expecting it, then surprisingly, he aims the same annoyed gaze at his daughter. "Morning."

A smile coasts breezily over her pretty pink lips as if blind to his cold shoulder. "Morning, Daddy."

I mumble a similar greeting, dipping my chin and sensing the sudden shift in the room. As if it wasn't already tense enough.

"Brooks, let's talk." He stares at his daughter, implying... I'm not sure what, and she looks as bewildered as I am. "In private."

She flinches, jaw dropping open as her eyes round. Something dark and pointed flickers in the depths of her sea-green eyes. Is it hurt? Anger?

I expect her to fight, tell her father she's staying put. But she says nothing, a little stunned and suddenly bereft. I'm desperate to fix whatever it is her father managed to do with just a look.

"Addie." Her name's an indulgence on my lips, sweet and savory.

It's brief and cutting as she casts a glance at me, filled

with shame or disappointment, and sadly, I recognize the sentiment all too easily. Then, just as quickly, a cold, impenetrable wall springs up between us.

Nodding tersely at her father, she twirls a full one-eighty, giving us her back, and flounces from the room.

"Sir, my apologies for just dropping in like this but..." I rub at the center of my chest.

George holds up a hand, slowly making his way to my end of the table. No words are spoken, but he makes it clear I'm in his seat. Feeling like a punished schoolboy, knuckles rapped and all, I avoid his gaze, standing quickly and vacating his chair.

"Brooks." He rests a hand on the table. "It won't come as any surprise, and I'm not one to speak evil of the dead, but I never liked your father."

He pauses, holding my gaze for what feels like a millennium. Internally, I battle not to squirm while I wait for him to continue.

"Devlin Kincaide was a ruthless, conniving man. I always believed he never had a heart, and no one could convince me otherwise."

Folding my arms across my chest, I mash my lips together, not able to argue with him but not wanting to hear it, all the same. I'm aware of my father's shortcomings, and I'm being kind in positioning it that way.

"The Kincaides and Monroes have never gotten along." My response is pat as I fail to keep my discomfort in check.

He's nothing like my Pa. There isn't a cold, stony demeanor to him, yet he isn't soft or a pushover. When he means business, it's clear in his firm stance, steady gaze, and square jaw.

George Monroe commands attention, but there's also something downright decent about him that makes me nervous, and how pathetic is that?

"You're a smart man so I'm sure you've figured out by now that I don't trust you or your motives where my daughter is concerned—"

I interject, "Sir—"

"Let me say my piece." He holds up a weathered hand. "I may not be happy with this arrangement, but such as it is, I'm willing to give you a chance. It'd be too easy to condemn you because of who you are, but I never did believe in the sins of the father and all that."

"I appreciate that, sir."

"But look here, Brooks. This is your one and only opportunity to prove me wrong. And if you fail me, or more specifically, fail Addie, I will make you regret the day you were born. I took a lot from your father and that was because it was between the two of us. But I won't be so generous where Addison is concerned. You hear me?"

I nod, ready to defend and respond, but he isn't finished. His sharp eyes tell me so.

"Show me you aren't like him. Prove you're better than that good-for-nothing son of a bitch ever was."

Speechless admiration and something I can't name bruise my chest. What do I say to a man who has every reason to distrust me and yet by withholding his judgement, he's giving me more of a chance than my father ever did?

8

ADDISON

*O**ur lives are entwined.*

Brooks's words circle my mind as I spoon steaming eggs and crisp bacon from the frying pan onto a plate. It's food I had no intention of cooking today, but just the slightest hint he's hungry and here I am, playing happy homemaker.

What kind of mess have I gotten myself into with this man?

My stomach dips, and my knees feel wobbly. How the hell am I going to keep myself from getting sucked in further?

Our deal was simple—we'd get married, he'd get control of his ranch, and we'd make my sustainability plan a reality. But with everything moving ahead so quickly, I didn't stop to think what all our marriage would entail or how it might change more than my last name.

Or how much I might want to sidestep my own rules and get naked with him.

And now he's talking about our lives being wound together like we're Romeo and freaking Juliet, and I'm cooking him breakfast while worrying how to stay out of his bed and keep him from digging his way under my skin.

I take a deep breath to steady myself.

This whole thing is moving too damn fast—no thanks to my libido. I just need to move us back a few steps and slow everything down. I need Brooks to understand where my priorities lie.

I may have been joking when I warned him not to fall in love with me, but us sharing a bed and living together is a little too close for comfort.

It'd be too easy for the lines to blur. For us to become more than shared interests and mutual respect. More than the sexual tension crackling in the air around us. A hell of a lot more than I bargained for.

And I don't like it one bit.

Because I am not my mama. I will not abandon this ranch or Daddy. Not for any reason.

With the plate of hot food in hand, I head for the dining room, hovering out of sight for only a moment. But not out of earshot.

"Yessir. I will," Brooks agrees—to what I'm not sure, but the idea of the two of them colluding behind my back has me biting at the inside of my lip.

"I sure hope so." Daddy's voice sounds strained, like he's holding something back. "For your own sake, and my daughter's."

These infuriating men. Between the two of them, I don't know who to be angrier with.

I square my shoulders and strut my ass into the room, head held high.

From the second my toes cross the threshold, Brooks's attention is on me. He's engrossed in my every movement, so I put a little extra swing in my hips for good measure. Then, with zero finesse and all my pent-up frustration, I drop the plate of food onto the scratched tabletop, causing the silverware to clatter and bits of egg to tumble off the plate.

Brooks says nothing but raises a single eyebrow my way. The look is both aggravating and ridiculously sexy, and I really wish he'd stop. It's hard to think straight when he's looking at me like that.

"Think I'll just take mine to go," Daddy says, picking a blueberry oatmeal muffin from the small plate of pastries I'd set out earlier. "Promised Missy I'd check in on her, anyway."

"Who's Missy?" Brooks asks with honest-to-goodness interest in his tone.

Like I'm going to fall for that.

"Cousin Hank's new horse." I drag out a chair, the legs scraping loudly against the wood floor, and motion for him to sit.

Brooks flashes my father one last hopeful glance, but Daddy's smarter than that. He knows my moods better than anyone, except maybe Hannah, and can tell when it's time to get out of my way. Muffin in hand, he scurries off as fast as his old bones will carry him.

Brooks sits as instructed, picks up his fork, and turning

his eyes to mine, smiles. It's a devilish, *two can play at this game* kind of smirk, and it makes me want to rip into him.

Or kiss him senseless.

Shit. Maybe the two of us alone together isn't the best idea. But Daddy's out the door before I can change my mind.

"You gonna join me?" Without waiting, he shovels a large bite of eggs into his mouth and rumbles a moan as he chews.

Dazed, I sit across from him, too angry and turned on to even consider eating. I watch in bitter awe as he gulps down the meal I made just for him.

My husband.

"So, Hank's been helping you out around here?" he asks, cutting through the tension.

"Yes." I find a spot on the scarred table to pick at, studiously avoiding his gaze. "Seems he's made himself comfortable, too. I'm not sure he's ever planning to leave."

"You want him to leave?"

It's a simple question, but the way he asks makes it sound like something so much more. He tilts his head just a bit, like he's working to figure me out, and layers his words with so much nuanced concern, it makes my insides feel like jelly.

"No," I admit. "I'm not sure I could hold this place together and look after Daddy all on my own."

"What do you mean, look after him?"

I sigh, my irritation long gone, replaced with a bone deep weariness. "He acts like nothing's wrong, and most of the time he seems fine. But he's not well, Brooks. He's not well, and it's only going to get worse..." I'm cut short by a sudden choke of tears, threatening to overwhelm me.

No further words required, he's out of his seat and kneeling at my side.

"Addie, darlin'." He takes my chin in his big, warm hand and gently forces me to meet his gaze.

"He's all I have." The words rush out in a tumble, my throat burning. "Him and this damn old ranch, and I can't lose either one. I won't."

Deep lines form with the pinch of his brow. "I'm sorry. I didn't know."

I shake my head, still unwilling to give in to the emotion but not trusting my voice to come out unbroken.

"Come here." He urges me toward him, guiding me into an embrace.

I lean into him, burrowing my face against his sturdiness, and allow him to pull me closer. And closer still. Until I'm in his lap and we're sitting on the dining room floor.

"I'm sorry," he repeats, his lips brushing my forehead.

I sniffle, still holding back the tears. "It's okay. I'm okay."

"Addie, I hardly know you, but even I can tell that's a lie."

I draw back to look at him, my eyes narrowing on his. "You cannot."

His finger runs a hot trail over my face, from my temple to my cheek, down across my jaw, and farther to the base of my neck.

"Your pulse, right here," he murmurs. "It's like a runaway stallion."

My heart pounds harder, and heat creeps across my skin as his long fingers splay wide, wrapping around my neck in a move that feels bold and possessive.

"And you do this thing with your mouth." His eyes grow

dark, and he brushes his thumb over the curve of my bottom lip.

"Brooks. I don't..." My thoughts are lost as he brings his mouth over mine.

The kiss is hard, hot, and all-consuming. He strokes his tongue into my mouth, and I let him, answering his low groan with a mewl of desire.

In an instant, I'm wet and aching, clinging to his broad shoulders and chasing his lips with mine.

God, how is he so good at this? How does he know what to say? Where to touch? When to move?

As if in answer to my thoughts, he shifts, bringing me along with him, and somehow, I find myself straddling him—his concrete body laid out beneath me, our mouths still fused together, and the only thing between his gloriously hard shaft and where I want him most is two layers of denim.

My need is overwhelming, and I can't help but grind shamelessly against him. It's not enough, yet it's so fucking good. I moan into his mouth, working my way into a frenzy.

But his hands are on my shoulders, driving me back instead of pulling me closer. Our mouths detach, and he pushes me off him—gentle but deliberate.

"Wait," he demands, his voice rough. "We can't. Not here. Not like this."

His eyes are large and regretful, and my racing heart stalls.

"No, of course. You're right." I shoot to my feet, swiping at the imaginary dust on my pants, and pretend to be unaffected by his rejection.

He's on his feet now, too, and trying to stop my needless fussing. "Addie, it's not like that."

Why does he have to sound so sincere while dumping cold water on my pride?

"Don't," I snap, not holding back the bite in my tone. "I do not want to hear how sorry you are. Not again."

He looks like he's ready to argue, but I can't deal with any more mood swings today—his or mine.

"Listen," I say, my body calming and my mind finally coming back online. "I think we can agree this was a mistake. So was last night. And it's not going to happen again."

He studies me a moment, his mouth opening and closing like he's not sure what he wants to say. I wait him out, my body trembling as the exhaustion resurfaces.

The problem is, I don't know what I *want* him to say.

Would it be better if he agreed? Do I want him to blame it on hormones and circumstance? Or do I want him to fight with me? For me?

"Whatever you want." His expression is unreadable, giving me no satisfaction.

I stifle a groan, realizing it's going to be a good long while before I'm properly satisfied again. If ever.

"I mean that," he continues. "But like you said before, this is a partnership. That means concessions on both sides, Addie. Give and take."

"Okay. What are we negotiating, exactly?"

"I can't live here full-time. This deal won't work if my family doesn't think I'm serious about running Canyon Spring. That means putting in face time and doing the work I've always done." He inches closer, slow and predatory.

I cross my arms, warding off the thrill of having him near. "Well, I can't live with you full-time, either. I've got a responsibility here, and I'm not about to run out on it."

"I don't expect that of you. Compromise, darlin'. We'll split our time half and half. Sound fair?"

"Yes, I guess so."

"Good. Now I gotta get to work, but we should start thinking about our green initiative and where we want to start."

"That's easy." I brighten, the topic lighting a new fire in my weary brain. "Solar fences."

"Really? I was thinking wastewater reduction."

Just when I thought we might actually be on the same page. "I've done my research, Brooks. You should trust my judgement."

"Trusting you and agreeing with you aren't the same thing. But in the spirit of making this *partnership* work, I might be willing to concede." He leans forward and gives me a quick peck on the cheek.

"Thank you," I mutter.

He pulls back from me but throws a cocky smirk my way. "Thank you for the breakfast, I appreciate it. I'd also appreciate seeing you at my dinner table tonight."

I open my mouth to argue, but he isn't done. "That's an expectation, darlin', not a request."

Mouth still agape, I watch him go and a thousand replies burn the tip of my tongue.

9

———

BROOKS

I park my truck out front, next to Addie's, and after a quick walk through the house, I'm back outside, scanning the Monroe ranch for any sign of her.

This morning at breakfast, we'd agreed to meet at Canyon Spring for dinner and for Addie's first night at my family home. Or more, I left before she could say otherwise. But the longer I thought about it, the less I trusted her to meet me there.

She isn't all too keen to be on my turf and among my family, and while I understand where she's coming from, it was part of the agreement. We'll split our time between the two ranches.

So, at lunch I sent a text, offering to ride over to my family home together after work. True to her sass and smarts, Addie saw right through what I'd hoped would come across as chivalry.

Addie: I'd like that, but don't think I don't see what you're doing.

Me: And what would that be?

Addie: Making sure I'm at Canyon Spring tonight. I said I'd be there. Don't you trust me, Brooks?

My response was an emphatic *of course I trusted her*, but now, with her nowhere in sight, the doubts are creeping back in. Did she change her mind? Is she hiding out and hoping I'll go on without her?

I jog toward the stable, figuring that's the next best place to look, and sure enough, Addie, George, and Hank are gathered around one of the horse stalls.

"I don't know, this isn't like her." Hank's worried tone matches the furrow on his brow.

"And when did she start doing this?" Addie glances over her shoulder at the sound of my approaching steps. "Brooks, is it time already?"

I nod as George and Hank turn, both dipping their heads in greeting.

"Yes, it is. What's going on? Something the matter?" I sidle up beside George, who's leaning on the wall, hands behind his back and looking smaller and more weary than usual.

Their gazes are fixed on a filly spilling and throwing her grain all over rather than eating it. She's agitated and nervous, ears pointed and head tossing from side to side.

"She's bullheaded, that's all it is." George isn't dismissive but more irritated, although it doesn't seem to be at the horse or the conversation.

"Sure, she has a mind of her own, but I don't think that's

it." Addie tilts her head to one side, giving Hank her full attention. "Has she eaten with the other horses before?"

"Only once or twice and not recently. Why?"

"Maybe she thinks another horse is going to steal it? Remember how Ace used to act." She waits for her cousin to meet her eye. "And that rascal's been known to try and snag another horse's food. Maybe he did the same to her and she's now keeping an eye out."

"Yeah, suppose that could be it." Hank scratches at the back of his neck. "I just don't get it. She didn't do it before today, and when I had her out, she was fussing with the bit and tossing her head. We got nothing done today. She was just difficult."

It's clear Hank's bothered. The filly is important to him, and he's stumped. I inch closer, taking a better look at the beauty. "What's her name?"

"Missy." Addie's eyes are on me now.

"You say she just started acting off today?" I slide my hand over the side of the railing, offering it to Missy if she wants to come check me out. She doesn't budge, and fed up with the food, steps back.

"Yeah. Although I wasn't around much the last couple of days since I was tending to the cattle, wrangling them and such."

"And how old is she, two? Two and a half?"

"Yes. Brooks, what are you thinkin'?" Hank's intent on the horse.

"My guess is it's her teeth."

"You think?" He takes another look at Missy.

"She could be shedding her baby teeth, or sometimes

extra teeth can be the problem. Missy could need a bit seat or teeth removed. I'd get it checked out."

"Sounds like Brooks has something going on in that head of his," George pipes up from beside me, winking and then twisting up his face as his shaky hand grabs onto my forearm for leverage.

He straightens awkwardly, hands behind his back once more, and at first, I'm humbled and awed at his compliment, even if it's wrapped in a joke at my expense.

I'm not used to my opinion being heard on the first go-around or even the tenth, and compliments are like unicorns where I come from. But any of the pride and merit I'm feeling is quickly swallowed by my concern.

Judging by George's uncomfortable stare, he didn't intend to touch me and it had nothing to do with his joke. He was using me for support, and it's on the tip of my tongue to ask him if he's okay, but we share a silent, weighted look.

He mutters a gruff thanks under his breath in such a way that I know not to say anything. "Hank, listen to Brooks. Get Missy a dental check-up." The old man shuffles toward the exit to the barn.

"Daddy?" Addie moves as if to follow, but her father shoos her away with a backward swipe of his hand, still moving toward the door.

"Thanks, Brooks. I'm going to set up an appointment right now." Hank beams at me like I've solved world hunger, and a warmth spreads through my chest, filling me with more of that validation I try not to need.

Without so much as a backward glance, Hank races toward the office at the other end of the stable.

"He's right, thank you." My wife smiles at me. "He's so good with the horses, but sometimes, like any of us, he can be too close to something or care too much to see other possibilities."

I nod and tighten my jaw at Addie, who isn't looking at me. Her gaze is fixed on the very path her father took, and like Hank not too long ago, she wears a shroud of worry.

Our talk at breakfast about her father comes back to me where I was left with the distinct impression that when she mentioned looking after him, she meant more than just aging.

I want to ask, but we're still getting to know each other, and if I did right now, Addie would clam up.

"You ready to go to dinner?" I lift her hand and place it into the crook of my arm.

"Let me get washed up."

We head to the house, and she doesn't take long to freshen up. She changes into a simple but sexy as hell summer dress, and we're on the road in no time flat.

There's still some time until dinner, and I drive us past my family home and farther onto the ranch.

"Where are we going?" She turns to look at me and points behind us. "Isn't dinner in the house?"

"It is, but I want to show you something."

"Okay, but Brooks, I don't want to be late for my first dinner with your family."

"We won't be. Promise." I gently squeeze her knee in reassurance, and while more than tempted to keep it there, I let my hand drop to the space between us.

Not too far from the operational buildings of the ranch, I

turn off onto a beaten path. If I didn't know every square foot of this property, I wouldn't know the dirt trail was a road.

"Where are you taking me?" She clutches the side of the seat as the truck bumps over the rocky terrain.

"Not much farther now."

And it isn't long before I'm parking the truck off to one side in a patch of flattened dirt, long since eroded by the vehicles we've parked here before.

She gets out of the truck before I make it around to her side. "What is this place?"

"It's my most favorite place on the ranch." I take her hand in mine and pull her along a trail into low lying greenery and a field of wildflowers.

Not too far from us, a deer breaks into a run at our presence, disappearing into the nearby trees. We clear to the other side of the foliage and there we find ourselves standing at the top of a grassy slope, leading down to a winding stream. The land is lush, and the majestic view of the snow-capped mountains steals my breath, every time.

"Brooks, it's beautiful." An impressed reverence, so like how I feel every time I'm here, is evident in her voice. "I can see why you love it."

"Yeah." I lead her to a large rock.

She sits and I slide in beside her, still holding her hand in mine. "When I was a teenager, I used to sneak out of the house at night and come here."

"You did? It's quite a trek. What did you do?"

"I'd just sit in the dark and soak up the sounds and smells."

"Seriously?" She angles her head in such a way as to grab hold of my gaze. Disbelief sparks in her irises.

"Yes. I did. Why do you find it so hard to believe?"

"I don't know. It seems so Zen and you're a..." She waves her hand up and down the length of me, and I hold my breath, wondering what's going to come out of her mouth next.

"A...cowboy."

"Yeah, and so? I can't appreciate or respect nature?" I tease, taking no offense to her incredulity.

"No, that isn't what I mean."

"Then what did you mean, Addison Monroe-Kincaide?"

Heat flares in her eyes at the mention of her new name, and she nibbles on her bottom lip while the fire in her gaze spreads to her cheeks.

"I heard all about the Kincaide parties during high school."

Her eyes glitter with mischief, and I chuckle, shaking my head at memories of my youth. All my life, I've known Addie. We've always been polite, and we've even been involved in group community projects together, but it's like we lived in two different worlds.

We couldn't be seen together, even if she did catch my eye more than once or twice. There was no way, not with the Kincaide and Monroe family feud over some stupid property line. So, she wouldn't know about the Kincaide parties or that we were nowhere near where they were held.

"Nope. Those were over on the other side of the ranch, by the canyon and close to the spring."

"So, you never brought girls here to make out?" There's a

hint of longing in her tone, and I get an odd pinch in my chest.

"No, again. I've never brought anyone here." I squeeze her hand. "Not until you."

"No one? Not even your brothers or sisters?"

"No. This is my place. I reckon' some of my siblings might know about it and may have even come here themselves, but I've never brought anyone. I like being alone here."

"Then why'd you bring me?"

"Because you're different—you're my wife and I want to share things with you. I want to know everything about you. What's your favorite place? Where do you go to be alone?"

She blushes and looks away, staring out into the distance, and I take the chance to look my fill.

The lemon-yellow sundress sets off her bronze skin, and her profile carries a dreamy expression, as if she's drifted off to someplace else. Someplace where she's happy and care-free. And I hope I have something to do with her expression.

"And I'd like to tell you those things—" She still isn't looking my way. "—in time." The words she tacks on to the end hurt a little, but I understand.

I'd never say it to her face, but she scares the shit out of me.

Never before have I cared so easily and most probably, foolishly, about another's well-being. And marriage or not, we're only just now getting to be friends. Or at least I hope we can become friends.

"It's so green, it gives me hope. Like greener prospects are ahead." Addie's still admiring the landscape as I do her, and it hits me.

"That's it."

"What is?" She swings her head toward me.

"The name of our sustainability initiative. Greener Prospects."

Her eyes widen, sparkling in what I hope is agreement. "Oh, I like it. You're right. I didn't think it would be that easy to come up with a name."

"Hey, don't be so doubtful. Look at us, already making plans and agreeing so quickly. How about we decide on where we should start?" I'm going for gold, seeing how easily we agreed on a name.

"All right. Like I mentioned before, we should start with solar fences. And before you object, solar is in abundance and easy to harness. Think of the renewable energy and the costs we'd save after the initial outlay."

"Hmmm, I've been thinking about solar since you mentioned it, and while that's all true, we should start with something we already have up and running. Like I said before—a water recycling program. We've got a small operation going on here at the ranch and we could just—"

"Brooks, just because it's up and running at Canyon Spring, that isn't a good enough reason to focus there and expand." She purses her lips and quietly studies me. "I thought we were going to do this together?"

"We are. Why do you say that?"

She shivers and shakes her head. "Nothing. I think we should both think on it some more. Meanwhile, we can plan the gala and continue this part of our discussion later."

"Absolutely. No decisions are being made today, and this is a good start." I slide an arm around her, rubbing my hand up and down her arm. At first, she stiffens, but it doesn't last long, and she sinks into me. "You're cold—we should head on in for dinner."

"Sounds good." Her expression softens, and she raises a hand to rest against my cheek. "Brooks, thanks for sharing this with me. It really is beautiful, and I think I understand you a little better now."

"What? You mean I'm no longer a rough-and-tumble cowboy?" I tease, pulling her toward the truck.

"No, you'll always be a cowboy, but I can tell you've got a soft side hidden under that rough exterior. I'm pretty sure your heart is at least coated in gold, if not completely made of it."

It's my turn to fix my eyes ahead, not sure how to respond to her observations and also liking a heck of a lot of what she thinks.

And even still, with all I don't know about her, I recognize something in her that's buried deep within me. She makes me want—and even believe—I could have it all.

Not only the ranch and the sustainability plan, preparing us for a prosperous future, but also her. Someone who wants the same things, someone at my side, sharing in a life we will build together.

10

ADDIE

rooks drives us toward the Kincaide family home, and for the first time since I agreed to his proposal, I'm starting to feel like this marriage bargain might not be the biggest mistake of my life.

Sure, things between us are still a little rocky—we can't seem to agree on much, and I get the sense he wants more from me than I'm comfortable giving—but he's done more to put us on equal ground in a single day than Derek ever did in the few months we were together. Hell, I'm not sure Derek or any of my other boyfriends even tried.

Maybe that's because there's more to Brooks Kincaide than meets the eye. Much more. And that's saying a lot, considering how darn fine he is to look at.

It gives me real hope we'll make a solid team, even if we still haven't agreed on where to start our sustainability initiative.

Greener Prospects.

I smile to myself as he pulls his truck up along the circular drive, thinking we might be on the verge of something great. Our business could be bigger and better than I ever planned, and I have the silly urge to pinch myself to make sure it's not a dream.

Goosebumps rise along the backs of my arms as we park behind a line of gleaming vehicles. I'd be in awe of how much money is sitting in the driveway if it weren't for the massive home in front of us.

From a distance, it looks large enough to pass for a resort hotel. Up close, it's downright intimidating.

"Don't move," Brooks insists, hopping out of the truck and trotting around to my side.

He opens my door and, without a word, lifts me down to the ground—his warm hands easily encircling my waist.

"Look at you, playing white knight." Heat creeps across my skin as I look up to find his sapphire eyes fixed on me. "But I'm not helpless, you know."

"Trust me, darlin', I'm well aware."

I step back and clear my throat, brushing his hands away.

It would be too easy to lean into him right now. To stand on my toes and press my lips to his. To run my hands over his muscled torso...and other places.

Oh yes, it would be so easy. I could get carried very, very far away with this man.

But that's not part of our deal.

No matter how good it feels to be close to him, to have his hands on me, or how many secret spaces he feels like sharing, I can't fool myself into thinking this is anything more than a contract.

An agreement with an inevitable end.

"Ready to face the firing squad?" he jokes, leading me up the front steps to his home.

At least, I hope he's only kidding. Although, the closer we get, the faster my heart races. With the sweep of a hand, he opens the door and invites me to cross into enemy territory.

Daddy would laugh if he could see me now—hands clasped demurely, a polite smile pasted on, and my eyes bugging out of my head at the sheer size and elegance of the foyer.

I mean...damn. I know the Kincaides have money, it's just a whole other rodeo to see the extravagance so up close and personal.

"You good?" He nudges me, encouraging me to move farther into the open living space which is full of buttery-leather seating, warm wood beams, and the largest stone fireplace I've ever seen.

"Sure. I'm great. Hungry. But great. Actually, I'm starving. But great." God, I sound like a moron.

"Guess we better feed you, then." He chuckles. "Come on, darlin', let's go meet the family and see what's on tonight's menu."

I follow him to the back of the house, where floor-to-ceiling windows showcase another gorgeous view of the property. I stall briefly, gaping at the swath of little black dots spread across the valley.

"Not as nice a view as the one I showed you earlier, but Pa sure liked it. He always wanted to look out over the herd. I think he relished the feeling of control it gave him."

We stand in silence for a moment, watching the cattle

roam in the distance, and I shiver, imagining the shadow of Devlin Kincaide lording over us.

"Addison. Brooks," Trey mumbles as he approaches.

Brooks turns to his cousin with a curt nod. "Trey."

"Hi, Trey. It's nice to see you. It's been a long time." I shiver again as his eyes travel over me, assessing. "Well, other than the wedding, I guess."

"Yeah, and you're looking beautiful, as always."

A flush of embarrassment sweeps over me, but I cover it with an unladylike snort of amusement. "Thanks."

"You two know each other?" Brooks's tone is gruff, and if I'm not mistaken, tinted with jealousy.

"Of course." The corner of Trey's lip twitches.

"We're the same age," I explain, when they do nothing more than stare menacingly at each other. "We were in school together most years. Graduated in the same class."

Brooks grunts his understanding, but his gaze remains fixed on his cousin, even as Trey's eyes flash back to mine.

Trey isn't an expressive guy, and we don't know each other well. In fact, I don't know much about his life before he was adopted by Brooks's parents. Which is odd, considering the consistent churn of the Prospect gossip mill.

But he's always been the silent, brooding type.

As a kid, he sat at the back of the class and, despite knowing all the answers, never gave them unless called on. And given the history between our families, we weren't exactly friends.

Still, as impossible as he may be to read, I get the sense he's enjoying this moment and making his brother squirm.

"We were just going to dinner." I reach for Brooks's hand,

reminding him I'm still on his side—whatever that means.

A fine line forms in Trey's brow. "Dinner's done. Mama and Ridge had a meeting in town, and they're still out. The rest of us ate when we got hungry."

Brooks's hand flexes in mine. "Fine, we'll make our own."

"Don't let Mama hear about it," Trey warns.

"Of course not."

"Night, then." He offers a half smile as he passes, leaving Brooks and me alone once again.

"What did he mean, not to let your mother know...about what, exactly?"

He looks at our joined hands, his thumb running over mine, and I'm reminded again how easily the lines of this relationship could blur.

"We have a world class chef on staff." His lips twist to a sneer. "She wants to get our money's worth, which means no one's allowed in the kitchen for so much as a glass of water."

"Oh." What else is there to say? I've never felt so far out of my league in all my life, and I can't imagine what it was like to grow up in this house.

Maybe it's the obvious shock on my face or the nervous tremble of my hand, but Brooks's expression softens.

"Don't worry." He tugs me gently toward him, looping his arm over my shoulders and guiding me toward the kitchen. "What she doesn't know won't hurt her. Or us."

Something about the way he says "us" loosens the knot in my stomach. Like we really are a team, and together we can take on any challenge—even the likes of Sage Kincaide, who obviously didn't disclose her plans for this evening and left Brooks to look like a fool in front of his new bride.

Good thing appearances aren't what count with me.

The kitchen, like the rest of the house, is ridiculously oversized, and I giggle, wondering if I'd even know what to do with appliances this modern and counter space so large.

"Do you know how to cook?" I tease, poking Brooks in his side.

"Not really." He laughs, jumping when my fingers find a sensitive spot along his ribs. "But I can make a hell of a sandwich."

"Ohhh, sandwiches." My smile widens, and I continue provoking him with another stab of my finger, appreciating the playful glint it brings to his eyes.

He laughs harder and seizes my wrist, putting an end to my lighthearted torture.

"You better watch yourself, darlin'." His voice is deep and growly and makes my body hum.

"Or what?"

His smile turns predatory, and suddenly I find myself trapped between a wall of brick at my back and a wall of man at my front.

I struggle for breath as the air around us grows thick with heat.

"Or else."

Awareness sparks to life in every fiber of my being as his broad hand carves a slow path down my side. His parted lips hover over mine, and his fingers dance around my waist, taking their sweet-ass time, taunting me with his devious touch.

Who knew the hip bone was an erogenous zone?

Fuck, who am I kidding? My entire body is a livewire under his touch.

"Brooks," I pant, my hands fisting in his shirt.

He wets his lips, and I'm ready to climb him like a tree and beg him to fuck me, right here in his family's industrial-sized kitchen.

"Please."

"Please what?"

I open my mouth but can't force myself to say what I want. Because dammit...I'm not supposed to want this. Am I?

"Please back off," I whisper, releasing my hold on him and praying he does the same for me.

His head dips, and I gasp as he runs his lips over the shell of my ear.

"Why?" he murmurs, his mouth blazing against my skin. "You worried I'm going to seek revenge?"

"Wha—" My breath is stolen when he attacks. His fingers tickle up and down my ribcage, his sultry hold turning to a punishing assault.

Laughter echoes through the cavernous room—his and mine—and I wriggle, trying to get out of his hold. But he's relentless.

"Stop!" I cry, laughing so hard, I've got tears leaking. "Stop or I'm gonna wet myself."

"Oh, damn." He immediately backs off with his hands raised in surrender and wearing a huge, shit-eating grin. "Didn't realize I was dealing with a weak bladder."

My hands hit my hips and I square off with him. "I do not have a weak bladder."

"Nah, you can't fool me. I've finally seen a scratch

beneath your surface. Addison Monroe-Kincaide's not perfect after all. I'm going to remember this."

My chest heaves, and I labor to catch my breath. I'm winded, not only from our antics, but from the blow he just delivered.

"I never said I was perfect," I argue. "Never acted like I was, either."

"I know." He takes my hand, wrestling it away from my waist and forcing me closer. "I didn't mean it like that."

"How did you mean it?" I pin him with my most ferocious stare.

But he doesn't dissolve or back down. He returns my gaze with a fierceness of his own and leans in just a little closer.

"If I'm being honest, it's almost like you're too good to be true. Who'd have thought I'd end up married to a woman who seems so perfect for me? Guess I'm just looking for the holes."

"You mean, I make a better business partner than you expected?"

"Exactly." He drops my hand and my gaze and plasters on the most fake smile I've ever seen. "Time to impress you with my fabulous sandwich making skills."

I return his forced enthusiasm with an equally good show of contrived zeal, encouraging him to give it his best shot. I fluff off our deep moment with a smile and a laugh, pretending the emotions brewing within me are nothing more than misplaced lust and admiration.

Because that's all this is, right? I can't possibly have real feelings for him. We've only been married a day. And we've already agreed on how it will end.

No blurred lines. No feelings. No sex.

Those were my rules. Now I just need to stick to them.

After our meal of savory roast beef on rye sandwiches, Brooks shows me through the rest of the house. It's a maze of finely furnished rooms which all seem cold and unwelcoming, and I wonder how much of my time I'm going to have to sacrifice here.

"Need anything before we head for bed?" Brooks asks as we meander down an empty hall.

I stop dead in my tracks. "Bed?"

He turns to me with a wide grin. "Don't worry, Addie, it's been a long day and there's another coming just 'round the corner. All I want is some sleep."

As though his statement settles it, he turns and continues down the hall, forcing me to jog to catch up.

"Is there a room for me?"

"There sure is." He opens a door, flicks on the light, and ushers me in. "You can sleep in here."

The walls are a light cream color, with dark curtains and a large navy rug over wide-planked oak floors. There's a king size sleigh bed decked with navy and cream bedding in the middle of the room, a gorgeous, distressed dresser on one wall, and an overflowing bookcase against another.

It's spacious, yet cozy. The kind of room I could picture myself snuggling into each night.

The door closes behind me, and I turn, wondering why Brooks didn't bother to say goodnight. But he's standing there, his back against the door, watching me.

"This is your room?" I squeak.

His chuckle is low and deep. "Of course it is, darlin'.

We're married. You think my family's going to give up a room so you can have a space all your own?"

"I guess not." I shake my head, not sure what to think. "But I didn't bring anything with me. I'm not sleeping naked with you."

This time his laugh is full and loud. "Hell no, you're not. Sorry, but there's no way I'd be keeping to my side of the bed if you were taunting me with that body in all its natural glory."

He steps around me to the dresser and shuffles through a drawer before tossing an oversized T-shirt my way. "Here. You can have this one to keep."

"Thanks," I mutter, relishing the feel of the soft, worn fabric between my fingers.

We take turns in his private bathroom, then hesitantly, I crawl into his bed.

As expected, it's the most comfortable mattress in the world—a million times better than my own—and I'm immediately at ease.

Brooks clambers in beside me, and even though his big body takes up a lot of space, he keeps a respectable distance. I lie in silence, wondering how the hell this thing between us grew into something so big, so fast. I don't know what it is. Or if it's even real. I just know I'm more terrified than I've ever been.

Rolling to my side, I try to push away the doubts. Or at least hide from them for a while. "Goodnight, Brooks," I murmur into the darkness.

He rolls toward me, snakes an arm over my waist, and kisses the top of my head. "Night, my darlin' little wife."

11

BROOKS

Side by side, Addie and I walk from the stable to my house for dinner. The sun, no longer blinding, is a paler yellow and lower in the sky, mixing with the warm hues of violet, hot pink, and orange sorbet.

Blonde hair in a braid down the middle of her back, she hangs her head as if fascinated with how every one of her steps annihilates a small mass of vibrant grass.

It's been a couple of weeks since that first night when I took her to my spot on the ranch and showed her how well we could fit together. And for the most part, we've gotten into a comfortable rhythm, straddling both our ranches and families.

"You're awful quiet. What's on your mind?" My arm brushes hers deliberately, and her thoughtful gaze finds mine.

"Hmm, nothing much. I was just wondering how long

we're going to keep this up." Glossy strands of gold hair fly around her face.

"Keep what up?" My fingers curl around her wrist to stop her.

Is she still having second thoughts about the marriage?

"This back and forth on where to start with Greener Prospects." Her hand slices through the air between us like an ax splitting wood. "We're running out of time. We've planned the hell out of the gala, but we still can't agree on the first step for the damn business. I really don't want to postpone the only thing we've agreed on."

"Hey, who said anything about delaying?" I grip her shoulders and soften my tone. "We're just having a healthy debate. I agree, we've got to make a decision soon, but we're not postponing the gala. I'm confident we'll get there."

We're still circling each other with our proposals of where best to start. I'm still solidly in the water recycling camp, and she won't budge from solar fences.

"Well, I'm glad one of us is." She wrestles out of my grasp, trying to sidestep me, but I'm quick, capturing her around the waist and pulling her back against my chest.

"Brooks," she shrieks, but there's no mettle to her protest when she quivers and burrows her warm, soft curves into me.

Palm splayed on her taut stomach, I dip my head closer to hers, and my lip grazes the soft spot just below her ear. She smells divine—floral feminine goodness. My throat dries and I want to stay like this for the rest of the night.

My eyes drink in her heaving chest, and I force my gaze to the sky. "Look at that sunset."

"It's beautiful." Her tone is yielding and reverent.

"That it is." Not quite sure if I'm talking about the globe in the sky or the fiery beauty in my arms.

The gold medallion in the sky is all majestic warmth, but that warmth is fleeting— like my wife is most days. And like a sunset, I wish I could say Addie's affability is at least a daily occurrence, but it would be a lie.

To be fair, some days there are long stretches of time where I'm able to breach the wall of her fortress. Where she is about to open up about her father and his health and the financial woes of their ailing ranch.

But I no sooner breach the top of said wall, believing we'll be more than a transaction, and she erects a secondary defense, hurtling me to the ground. *Thud.*

"What are you two up to? We run a respectable place here." Ridge's fake chirpiness, laugh and all, causes the hairs on the back of my neck to spike.

Addie leaps from my arms like we're teenagers caught making out and whirls around to face my brother. "We were just looking at the sunset."

The sky is now a deepening amethyst, fast shifting into stormy slate, and he casts an aloof glimpse above before dropping it on my wife. "Must be nice to have the time to watch the sun set."

I curl my hands around my belt to stop them from doing something destructive but wonderfully satisfying. Like cracking his nose.

"Was there something you wanted?" I rub the back of my neck, trying to ease the mounting tension.

"Did you call the ban—"

"Yes, and I already spoke to Charlie. It's all taken care of."

"Fine. Dinner is almost ready. You two should come in."

"We were on our way." Addie takes the lead toward the house. "Ridge, maybe you can help us settle a *debate* we're having."

The way she flings the word I used at me sets my teeth on edge, and now she's bringing my brother into this. She might as well wave a red flag in front of my face and make me the bull.

"What's that?" He quirks a brow, now thoroughly intrigued.

"We're trying to decide on our first sustainability project, and I think it should be solar fences." Her lip curls into a sly smile as if she's already won. Why does she see this as a competition?

"And what does Brooks want?" Ridge is many things but stupid isn't one of them. Like a shark smelling blood in the water, he's more than happy and eager to add to the carnage.

"He says wastewater reduction." She sways her hips. My balls tighten the way they always do when she moves, and it takes everything in me to tamp down my attraction.

"What I said was—"Pausing, I work my jaw and try to even out my tone."—either is a worthy pursuit and an excellent start out the gate, but a water recycling program would be a simpler and quicker win."

She opens her mouth, ready to knock me down, and Ridge is right behind her, a wicked gleam in his eye.

I ignore them and the ache in my chest that feels a lot like betrayal. "Think about it. Canyon Spring Ranch already has a recycling system in place."

Thanks to me, I think, but I don't comment because it is a small operation. It's all I could get away with without having to square off with Pa.

"We could build it on a larger scale with not a lot of financial outlay and see the benefits sooner."

Addie sniffs, pursing her lips, and Ridge's determination is a pointed spear. "I think we could say the same for either project in terms of the benefits. Your argument is weak, at best, Brooks."

Of course, you'd say that. Asshole.

"True," Addie chimes in, and an inkling of a smile brushes her lips.

"If so, what's the big deal with going with a water recycling program first?" I challenge, starting to walk again.

"Why are you so set on disagreeing with me?" She scampers to my side, and Ridge's snicker at my back causes me to stop.

"You know, Addie, Brooks was never that good at seeing the bigger picture." My brother is now in front of us, hands out at his sides like he's a leader or preacher. "All the opportunity our land offers. You and I should talk about this some more. I'm sure I could move this along and get results faster."

"I-I... No, I—" Flustered, she wrinkles her cute, pert nose, and regret splashes across her cheeks, an alluring shade of cherry red, visible even in the dark. "That's not what I meant by asking your opinion. Brooks and I can figure this out ourselves."

I cross my arms over my chest, unwilling to bail her out. This is her mess. Ridge doesn't hide his amusement, a wicked glint in his eye.

He may think he can move right on in and kick me out of this deal, but he's dead wrong. I made a bargain with Addie, and while she may be giving me a hard time, I can trust her.

Her phone rings and she's lightning fast, snatching it from her pocket. "Excuse me, I have to take this."

She holds up the phone, and I just make out Hank's name on the screen before she spins on her heel, away from us. Jaw set, I wait until she's no longer in earshot to stab my brother with a glare.

"What the hell do you think you're doing?" I'm in his face, our noses practically touching.

"Settle down, Brooks. I was riling her up. It's easy to do and entertaining." I want to wipe his self-righteous smirk right off his face.

"Leave her alone." I poke a finger into his chest. "Got it?"

"Forget about that." He's dismissive and lowers his voice. "We need to talk. It sounds like you don't have a handle on this."

The knot in my stomach twists tighter. "I can't fathom how you've come to that conclusion with all the shit you're stirring up."

"Well, tell me, where's Canyon Spring Ranch in all of this?"

"It's fifty-fifty. We're right alongside the Monroes." My gut spasms.

"That's what I thought you'd say, and that's where you're wrong. We both know it's our name and money making any of this possible."

That isn't entirely true. We will put up more capital, but

our ranch is larger, and in the long run, we'll make it all back and then some.

"As usual, you're not looking out for the ranch. You should be putting us first."

"What the hell are you talking about? Of course, I am. We're going to be leading sustainability in Prospect." A snarl tears from me and I clench my fists. "I already have the Clarks, Lenny Rhodes, and Hopper talking to me about getting in on it."

"Fine, but the Kincaide name needs to have top billing. None of this fifty-fifty shit." He glares at me. "You want Mama to see you as the rancher we need, then show us what you're made of."

He storms past Addie who is headed toward me. She stops, paling at something she sees in my face. Or maybe her call?

"Everything all right?" I dip my chin at the phone still in her hand.

"Yeah, fine. I just don't know how you live with these people. I can't eat here without getting indigestion, let alone sleep here. I can't stay here tonight."

How much did she hear of my conversation with Ridge?

"We agreed on splitting our time. Tonight, we're here."

Stress lines the corners of her mouth. "I know, but—"

"I tell you what." I draw her inside the house and into an alcove, away from prying eyes. "Go on upstairs. I'll give our excuses and have dinner sent up to our room."

Her features soften, and she rests a warm palm on my chest. "Thank you, Brooks."

Getting us out of dinner isn't hard. Except for a minor

inquisition from Mama, no one cares about our absence, and it makes me question why I insisted on being here.

When I get to the room, Addie prances from the bathroom in a towel. Like a deer in headlights, her eyes widen and lips part. Droplets of water sprinkle the tops of her creamy shoulders, and wet tendrils of hair hang around her face.

She flushes, half turning back to the privacy of the bathroom when I croak out, "Don't go. Relax; this is as much your space as it is mine."

"Brooks, I'm in a towel." She snorts, rolling her eyes, but a darling pink flush works its way up her chest and neck. And she doesn't move to escape or throw something over her body.

"And you're damn sexy. Never seen a towel look so good." I'm much closer now, not sure how I got within touching distance so fast. "It makes me want to get my hands on it. On *you*."

A warped part of me wants to lean in and fill my lungs with her lethal combination of feistiness and inhibition. Get high on it. On her. But I know myself and I won't be able to stop there. No way.

"Brooks." Damn, the way she says my name, soft and sultry, causes my balls to twitch.

Transfixed, I stare at her elegant neck, the swell of her chest where the towel knots in front, and her silky-smooth legs. I wet my lips, unable to stop imagining my tongue tracking its way along the ridge of her collarbone and down into the valley of her breasts.

Common sense flees, and I grab her by the arms,

crashing her body against mine as my lips crush against hers. She parts her lips, releasing a gratifying moan.

She presses her luscious tits into me, and her fingers dig into my sides, spurring on my arousal, and I feel her willingness and taste her desire. It's just a kiss, but so much more.

This kiss brims with a quiet hunger, an intense agony, and at the same time, a state of grace I've never experienced before.

Addie is the reason.

I'm just not sure if it's because she's making my dream a reality, helping me take my rightful spot at the head of the Kincaide family, or because I'm a horny bastard, or because of who she is, who she could be in my life.

12

ADDISON

Brooks kisses me like he's a drowning man and I'm his only lifeline.

His mouth is soft yet demanding. His tongue a hot invasion yet soothing comfort. His hands—those glorious, glorious hands—are arousing, yet also an anchor.

It's a heady, intoxicating mix and makes me want to throw away all sense and decorum and get lost in the moment, in this feeling, with him. *Of him.*

In his arms, I'm the wild, willful woman I'm meant to be. A free spirit.

And a fucking turned-on mess.

"Brooks," I gasp when his lips tear from mine to carve a path down the column of my neck.

"Hmm." The deep gravel of his voice vibrates across my collarbone, where his lips are firmly planted, kissing and sucking.

I should stop this. I should tell him to back the hell off

and let me dress in private. I should remind him, and myself, this was not part of our deal.

But the word that leaves my mouth doesn't come from my sensible side. "More," I urge, my hands pulling to relieve him of his shirt, my leg rubbing up his thigh.

His hold is firm, but he pushes me back, separating our bodies and creating distance between us. A whimper escapes me at the loss of his heat, and my fingers scramble to keep purchase.

"You sure that's what you want, darlin'?" I hear him, but my eyes are glued to his chest—the way it expands with each heavy breath, and the light dusting of dark hair which covers taut, golden skin.

I feel my head bob in agreement, aware of the movement, but not in control. I'm under a spell, mesmerized by the sticky pull of lust bubbling within me.

"Addie." His tone is sharp and pained, demanding my full attention. Long fingers tangle in my damp hair, drawing my gaze to his lush lips and molten eyes.

Never would I have believed something so cool could burn so brightly.

Not until this moment.

Not until Brooks Kincaide looked at me like he could love me.

Like this thing between us could be real.

Like he's ready to fuck me into oblivion, if only I say the word.

"Tell me what you want. Say it."

I melt, suddenly willing to have him take over any and every damn thing. "I-I want..." But I can't finish the sentence.

I'm breathless, my head spinning, and I don't know if this feeling is true or something I'll later regret.

"I don't want to decide. I don't want to think," I tell him honestly.

"Ah, darlin'." His tone softens. "I can fix that. Come here."

With our hands linked, I follow him to the bed, my legs shaking and body vibrating. He stops, turning to me with an unreadable expression, and I wait for what comes next for what feels like an eternity.

Slowly, he glides a finger over me, tracing a path across my lips and down my neck, to land between my breasts, hooking around the towel which still covers me.

His lips part, the towel falls away, and I'm suddenly naked before him.

"Lie down." His order is a lick of fire across my chilled skin.

I splay out, my limbs an invitation, my hair a wet web, and the blood in my veins thick as honey.

"You're so beautiful," he murmurs, dropping a knee to the bed and hovering over me. "I could stare at you forever."

The air compresses around us, and I gasp at the weight of it. At the weight of his words, and the way his eyes bore into me, revealing much more than bare skin.

Bare skin which is a sharp contrast to all the clothes he's still wearing—even with his shirt hanging open from my feeble attempt to undress him. The rough scratch of denim brushes my inner thigh, and the cool skim of a button runs across my breast, accentuating my nudity.

Something about being exposed to him this way—being

vulnerable to him—turns me on even more. I'm practically crawling out of my skin with hungry need.

His lips sweep across mine briefly before tracking down my body. Hot, open-mouthed kisses land on my neck, my shoulder, my breast. A quick suck of a nipple. A sharp bite at my navel. Then a long, slow lick up my center.

A zap of pleasure shoots through me and I cry out, so overwhelmed, I forget where we are and who might overhear.

He licks and sucks and fucks me with his fingers, burying his face into my folds.

Each time I groan, he grunts in return, like he's enjoying this as much as I am. Shamelessly, I grind myself harder against him, until the sharp edge of orgasm curls around me, threatening to pull me under to bliss.

"Yes," he growls, still fingering me—the wet sound of my arousal turning me inside out. "Don't hold back. Give it to me, darlin'."

He latches onto my clit, sucking hard, and the orgasm slams into me, tearing apart the final shred of my control and squeezing a howl of pleasure from my soul. Wave after wave of pulsing euphoria thrum through me, liquifying my limbs and drowning me in a pool of rapture.

Brooks moans, deep and satisfied sounding, his hands still gripping me as he nuzzles his face to my belly.

"That was..." There are no words. Has sex ever been this good? And that was just his mouth.

"Perfection." He climbs onto the bed, pulling the blanket over us, and cuddles me into his warmth.

I know I should reciprocate—it seems only fair—but I'm

completely wrung out and can already feel myself getting sucked down into sleep. He murmurs into my hair. I can't make out what he's said, but it's soothing all the same.

This wasn't meant to happen. None of it. Not the marriage, the attraction, and certainly not the hot as sin gratification he just delivered. It should feel like a mistake.

But it doesn't.

It may be the endorphin high talking, but it feels a bit like fate.

❧

"You almost ready?" Brooks calls from the other side of the bathroom door.

My heart skitters to life—a strange new occurrence since our *intimate* moment, three nights ago. A night I've studiously avoided discussing and haven't dared request a repeat of.

Even though my body's screaming for an encore.

I answer by swinging the door wide and stepping out in a flourish, showing off the new dress he surprised me with this morning.

His mouth drops slack, and his eyes heat as he takes me in. I twirl, lifting the skirt to flash more of my legs.

When he doesn't say anything, I stop, hands on my hips. "Well?"

"I'm speechless."

"I'll take that as a good thing. But do you think it's right for dinner with your mother?" It's an expensive dress—nicer than anything in my closet—and I love the way the violet silk fits, skimming over my curves and swirling around my knees. But I'm still not convinced it'll be good enough for Sage.

Although, perhaps the fear's not so much about the dress as it is her acceptance of me. Not that I should care. I've never put much stock into the opinions of others, but it sure would make this whole marriage contract a heck of a lot more convenient.

And something tells me, it would make Brooks feel better, too.

"You're perfect," he assures me. "Let's go."

Our drive is mostly silent. Brooks is attentive to the road, but I'm transfixed by his hands on the wheel, imagining them on my body instead.

"There's something I've been meaning to ask you." His gaze darts toward me and away again.

"What?" I smile, hoping his mind's wandering the same territory as mine.

"Greener Prospects is coming together nicely, and we've got more local ranches interested in coming on board than I'd expected." He hesitates, his nostrils flaring, and I can see my world's about to close in.

"But?" I prod, anxious for him to get to his point.

"I just wonder if we couldn't do even better. Maybe if the Kincaide name was more prominent..."

Ice coils its way through me, chilling my blood and erecting a barrier around my heart. "You want to push me out and take over my plan?"

"What?" His head snaps to me, the truck jerking sideways with the movement before he quickly course corrects. "Fuck," he pants, pulling us safely to the side of the road.

But now that we're parked, he refuses to look at me. Refuses to say another word.

Well, fuck this. I'm not going to wait for this thing to implode. Maybe it's better to leave and end it now, before it's too late. It's going to end at some point anyway. Right?

I reach for the door handle, resolved to leave him before things get too far out of hand, determined I'll make my way back home on foot. Nothing and no one can convince me it's not the best option—even in this ridiculously fancy dress.

"Addison." His voice is flat but exacting. "Stay."

"Why should I?"

"Because that's not at all what I meant. It's not even what I want." He sighs, slumping back into his seat and digging his fingers into his hair.

I wait out his explanation. *It better be a damn good one.*

"I'm trying to think to the future. To do what's best for us both." He pulls at his hair, fingers flexing. "I know we agreed to equal billing, I just wondered if we'd be further ahead with the Kincaide name on top."

Not good enough. Not at all. "Sounds like a takeover to me."

He shifts in his seat, turning to grace me with his solemn stare. "I don't want to take anything away from you, darlin'. I want to make your dreams come true."

The ice thaws, just a bit, and my hands unfurl from the tight fists I've unconsciously made.

I want to believe him. I want to trust the sincerity in his tone and the longing in his gaze, but I'm too afraid he'll run away with my dream in his hands. Or more if I let him.

"We better get back on the road or we'll be late to

dinner." I turn away from him, searching for some sort of truth on the horizon.

We aren't late, but we are the last to arrive.

Sage, in a sophisticated black and white dress, sits across from my father who's wearing the same old suit as he did to our wedding.

Brooks and I are forced to sit opposite each other, at their sides.

Probably a good thing, since being too close to Brooks right now might trigger me to do something unfortunate. Like punch him in the junk for even suggesting our partnership be anything less than fifty-fifty.

"We ordered for you," Sage states with an air of indifference as we take our seats.

"Already?" Brooks frowns. "Didn't we agree to seven?"

"No." She lifts her chin higher, glacier eyes drilling into me. "The reservation was for six thirty."

It's a lie. I can see it in the roll of her lips and hear it in the way she subtly clears her throat. But why?

"I was late, too. Just got here," Daddy drawls. "We must've all got our wires crossed."

Sage flashes him a look of abhorrence, like she can't believe he has the audacity to speak, let alone contradict her in any way. "Yes, well, not surprising given you Monroes always tend to get things wrong."

"What's that now?" Daddy leans in, challenge clear in his tone.

"You and your daughter," Sage continues, seemingly unaware of the dangerous ground she's treading. "Neither of you seem overly capable."

"Capable?" Daddy's voice drops low. "I may be slowing down in my age, but Addie's twice the rancher I ever was. She'll be running circles round you and your boy."

"High-strung isn't the same as capable," she sneers. "As for you, well...it's no wonder Maribelle's no longer in the picture."

Daddy's face drains of color at the mention of my mother's name. He sits back, hands clasped rigid on the table in front of him.

"Enough," Brooks growls, slapping the table for emphasis.

Sage jumps at his outburst, but the movement is so subtle it's practically microscopic, making me wonder if I imagined it. She turns to him with a look of haughty arrogance, and I'm sure she's ready to lay into him.

"I have your drinks," the waiter announces, his gaze bouncing around our group, perhaps looking to see who's least likely to rip him a new one for interrupting.

"You may serve them." Sage nods, giving him permission to do his job.

The look on Brooks's face is pure torment, and I realize he's got a much bigger hill to climb if he wants the controlling seat of his family ranch. Is it even possible?

And more importantly...is it worth it?

It all seems like too much.

Too much pressure. Too much tension. Too much emotional manipulation for me to handle and remain polite.

"Excuse me," I mumble, reaching to give Daddy's hand a quick squeeze before extracting myself from the table and heading toward the restrooms.

I don't need the facilities; I just need a moment away from the overexaggerated drama and to collect myself.

After splashing cold water on my face and neck and giving myself a mental pep talk in the mirror, I finally feel more centered. More in control. If Sage Kincaide thinks she can scare me off with a few wicked words, she's sorely underestimated me.

But when I exit the restroom, I'm smacked with a new challenge.

Derek waits, leaning against the wall with his arms folded and a look of bitter resentment marring his otherwise attractive features.

"Derek. What are you doing here, standing outside the ladies' room?"

"I've got a better question," he taunts, dropping his arms and taking a menacing step toward me. "How the fuck did you end up married to Brooks Kincaide?"

Shit.

I did not see this coming. Or maybe I did—just not with this level of hostility and me cornered in a deserted hallway.

"It's not what you think," I stammer, and he takes another ominous step in my direction. "I can explain."

He doesn't stop his threatening approach until he's right in my face. We're up close and personal now, but nothing about this situation is reminiscent of the cozy times we spent together in the past. I want to run or knee him in the balls, but my stupid fancy dress wasn't built for that.

"How can it be anything other than exactly what it looks like?" he snarls.

I move backward, hitting the closed door behind me, just as a shadow appears at the end of the hall.

Unaware of our audience, Derek continues, "You're nothing but a two-timing, frigid, lying bitch, Addison."

My heart races out of control, my head twisting away from Derek's fury, to see my savior emerge from the shadows.

Brooks stalks forward, his face set with a stormy intensity. "Get the fuck away from my wife."

13

BROOKS

Fury boils its way up my spine. Derek Walton. Her ex is in her face, looming over her. I don't like the idea of any man other than me that close to my wife, and I don't care the reason.

Wild eyes glued to me, he straightens, taking a step back, but not far enough nor good enough for me. I stride to where they stand, clenching my fists as tightly as my jaw.

Addie's frozen, still resting against the door, more shocked than scared—and maybe excited? Her eyes are bright and round, lush lips slightly parted, and the prettiest pink I've ever seen paints her delicate cheekbones.

"Don't ever talk to my wife that way again." I glare at him.

The pupils of his beady eyes flare, and he takes another step back. This time, he widens his stance and raises his head so his pointy chin juts out.

"Step aside and let her pass." I lean into him and growl, "Or better yet, get lost."

The asshole sneers, pulling at the collar of his shirt and pumping out his chest as if that makes him more of a man. He can't help himself and steals another glance at Addie.

That's when I see it, the hurt with a touch of anger—or is it wounded pride—in the man's eyes. He storms away and she watches me, her expression more agitated now.

Fucking hell.

Don't tell me he's jealous or worse, going to make things difficult for us. And how does Addie feel about her ex? Does she still have feelings for him? Is she pissed I interrupted their little gathering?

"You all right?" My voice is rougher than I intend.

"Fine." She nods curtly. "I had it handled." Her slender hand runs absent-mindedly along the bodice of her dress, and I don't miss the slight tremble to her fingers.

"No doubt you did. But as your husband, it's my duty to protect you." I hold up a hand before she steamrolls me. "Or to have your back when you're sparring."

"Well, thank you." Her cheeks darken to a rosy red, and she avoids my gaze, casting her eyes down the darkened hallway in the direction of the dining room. "We should get back."

"Am I going to have to worry about him?" I inch closer, breathing in her sweet scent.

"What? Derek?" Her voice wavers as if she isn't so sure. "No. Not at all. You're not jealous are you, Brooks?"

"No, darlin'." I now press against her. Her firm tits poke into my chest, and her warm, sweet breath lingers at the base of my throat. "I'm not jealous, and do you want to know why?"

My forearms rest against the wall on either side of her head, caging her in. Addie's pupils dilate, and her lips form a small, tantalizing 'O'. My balls twitch as I imagine her mouth wrapped around my cock.

Aw, hell, now isn't the time.

"Why?" It's a coy whisper and she bats her lashes. I can't tell if it's an act or if she's as turned on as I am.

"Because, darlin', as soon as you saw me, nothing and no one else mattered." I trail a finger down the side of her face, tracing the angle of her jaw all the way to her pouty mouth.

My thumb presses into her bottom lip and she shivers, rubbing her legs together. I love how fucking responsive she is. Her need and desire splash across her features. Why'd I ever think she was acting?

"And Addie, in case you were wondering, I feel the same way." Removing my thumb, I pinch her chin and bend my head, tongue flicking at her plump bottom lip, and without any effort she opens, letting me in.

"Brooks." My name is both a tortured and tantalizing moan, teasing all my nerve endings as my lips crush hers.

Kissing her softly, slowly with closed lips, alternating to deep, hard open-mouthed kisses, I lose myself in the feel of her warm mouth. My tongue circles hers, and my fingers dig into the wall, itching to touch her, have her.

I want to feel the smooth elegant sweep of her neck, the tight, hardened peaks of her breasts, and the soft curve of her waist. Damn, I want to feel every inch of her even through the too many layers of our clothes.

"I should take you right here. Make sure Derek and

everyone else understands you're with me. You're mine and I'm yours."

She sucks in a breath, fingers curling into the sides of my waist. She likes the sound of that.

"Can you imagine me balls deep inside of you? My cock filling you. Addie, I promise you, I'll make you scream my name when you come."

How she lost herself in my bed days ago floods my mind. The musky alluring smell of her arousal, those sensational cock-hardening moans. Fuck, I'm going to come just thinking about getting her off again.

I grind my rock-hard cock between her legs, where I'm sure she's wet for me. My fingers pulse and ache to slide through what are sure to be hot, slick folds and plunge into her core.

She arches her neck, hands flying to my head where her fingers dive into my hair. Nails scrape along my scalp with enough pressure to lightly score the skin. Burning tingles of pleasure shoot to my groin, and the loud clatter of a dish hitting the floor behind us is like a bucket of ice water dumped on my head.

I stiffen but not in a good or arousing way. We are in a public place. Addie deserves better than this. And if anyone sees us like this, or worse, if Sage Kincaide were to catch wind of this, just think of the scandal. That's what she'd say. Oh, yeah, there'd be hell to pay.

I force myself to pull away from her but not fully—just enough to breathe, clear my mind, and form a coherent thought. "We should get back before Mama sends a search party."

"What?" She blinks a few times, slowly coming out of her lustful daze, and like me, she starts to fix her neckline as her fingers brush at her hair.

"You ready to go face the monster?" My lips slide into a lopsided smile, and I smooth a stray strand from her face.

"Brooks, you did not just call your mother a monster?" Her tone is mock-shock and her lips smash together, holding back a grin.

"Do you have a better name for her?"

She laughs, shaking her head, but it's plain to see she's being polite and is sure to have a few choice names for my mother. Don't we all.

"Let's go. Once we're done with our entrées, we're out of here, and we'll take your father too."

"Now you're talking." She loops her arm in mine, and we march back to the table.

Poor George looks ready to kill my mother, knuckles white as his fingers hold his knife and fork like weapons ready to spear her. His shoulders relax a little at our return, and Mother ignores us for the first little bit. That suits me just fine.

Dinner is unappetizing. Well, the food is delicious, but I don't enjoy a bite. And when even as promised, I cut the meal short, it still feels like it was too long an evening thanks to Mama's presence.

On the drive home, this time to Addie's place, we sit in comfortable silence, both wrapped up in our own thoughts. Tonight started badly and all because of me.

I had to open my big mouth and foolishly do Ridge's bidding. Why the hell did I even suggest the Kincaide name get top billing on our green ranching initiative? Why didn't I stick to my guns and say nothing? It wasn't a lie when I told Ridge it didn't matter and would make no difference.

Canyon Spring Ranch stands to gain a lot from this, and it'll only strengthen our reputation. Just look at the other ranches already clamoring to get on board and looking to us to lead. That fact alone proves that whoever's name is first on the promotional material is insignificant.

The look on Addie's face when I dared to suggest it—it was enough to make me want to punch myself in the dick. I'd have been spitting nails if she said the same bullshit to me.

Yeah, the night had gotten off to a rotten start, and things didn't get any better when Mama had to be her usual charming self, slinging insults and making her power plays. Thankfully, all that is behind us.

As I steer us into a spot outside Addie's home, she sighs and turns to me. "Brooks, thank you for dinner. I dreaded tonight for many reasons..."

She looks out the windshield at her father meandering up the walk to the front door. He's a little unsteady on his feet, and it has nothing to do with alcohol. He didn't drink a drop at dinner. She did say he isn't well. I should help her, help George, with that.

"But you made it bearable," she whispers, still staring straight ahead. "And as for Derek, I meant what I said. He isn't a problem."

"You're welcome, and I'm glad to hear it."

We get out and I meet her at the front of the truck, taking her hand in mine as we make our way inside. George is hobbling around at the entrance, almost as if he's waiting for us.

He busies himself with a stack of papers, looking up to capture Addie's attention. They share a look and a silent conversation in a matter of moments.

"Well, good night, Daddy." She kisses his cheek and makes her way to the staircase. "I'll see you upstairs, Brooks."

I stare after her, enthralled by the seductive sway of her hips and the sensual curve of her ass. I want to follow but sense George has something on his mind.

No surprise. This will be a lecture or tongue-lashing for Mama's behavior. It has to be. I'm pissed, and I wasn't the one she took shots at all night.

"You did right by Addie and me tonight," he rasps, dropping the papers and envelopes back onto the table. "Thank you."

"No need to thank me." I'm quick to cover my surprise with a neutral expression. "As I'm sure you've figured out for yourself, my mother isn't an easy woman to like...or love."

He harrumphs in agreement, sidling up beside me.

"If I could have spared you the entire ordeal, I would have, but it was inevitable."

"Oh, I know. It's just as well, we got it over with and survived to tell the tale." He chuckles and it morphs into more of a wheeze.

I want to ask him about his health, see how I can help, but I could wind up insulting him. Addie's been cryptic, and I don't know if it's just aging or something worse.

"Do you like to fish?" His out of the blue question pulls me back to our conversation.

"Is that even a question?" I jest, removing my jacket and folding it over an arm. "Of course, I do."

"Good." A wrinkled grin creeps across his face, and he nods once. "See you at five a.m."

"I beg your pardon?"

"Tomorrow morning, I'll meet you in this very spot." He thumps the banister of the staircase. "Coffee'll be hot and ready, and we'll have breakfast to go. We gotta get out there while the fish are biting."

He ambles past me but pauses on his way down the hall, casting a glance over his shoulder at me. "Good night, Brooks."

Well, what am I supposed to do with this? George Monroe, my father's enemy, new father-in-law, and practically a stranger, is taking me fishing.

"Night, George."

A weird tightening and warming starts in the center of my chest and spreads from there, making me both uncomfortable and oddly pleased. The stretching of my cheeks and crinkling of my gaze gives me pause.

Damn, I'm smiling. Even with all the bullshit tonight, I'm happy.

Could this be my life?

A beautiful woman at my side and in my bed every night, and not just any woman, but Addison Monroe-Kincaide. A woman just as smart, passionate, and beautiful as she is driven to make her dreams come true. Just being with her makes me want to be a better man. A man she deserves.

And George. A father-in-law who might respect me. A man who could be more of a father to me than my own.

Together, we're a family.

A family who accepts me, includes me, and wants to spend time with me.

If this is my life, I don't want anything to change. I want to do everything in my power to make this work. To turn this agreement I've struck with Addie into the real deal.

14

ADDISON

The smell of two of my favorite things, coffee and burnt bacon, wakes me. I inhale the rich aroma, appreciating how it mingles with the woodsy scent of Brooks's body wash, which now takes up sensory residence in my bed.

God, he smells good.

But when I ghost my hand over the spot where he should be—the spot he's inhabited every night since our wedding—I come up empty.

Not surprising, really. He's pulling double or maybe even triple time, upholding his duty at Canyon Spring Ranch, building our business and planning for the gala, plus helping Hank with our horses in his spare time—a chore he seems especially fond of.

He's also been up before dawn each day, squeezing in time with Daddy before heading out for work. It's nice to see them getting along and to know Daddy's no longer holding a grudge.

Still, I miss having Brooks's big body here beside me.

Now, if only I could figure out how to get other *big* parts of him *inside* me, I'd be a happy, happy woman.

I was a fool to think the attraction between us could be ignored or boxed in by the lines of a business contract. He's too honest, too loyal, too damn sexy to evade. And he likes me—or at least, he seems to respect me, which is a hell of a lot more than I can say for most of the men I've dated.

Brooks is different, and I crave that. I crave him. Crave the feel of his lips, his tongue, his touch.

Unfortunately, he seems intent on keeping my ridiculous rules in place.

I can't figure out why, but something changed after our dinner with his mother last week, and despite his incredibly hot and dirty promise to make me scream his name—a promise I have no doubt he's very capable of keeping—our physical relationship has stalled.

Only, the sexual tension is still there, thick as always. It pulls between us like barbed wire, trapping us together, and cutting deeper the more we try to break free.

And it's driving me crazy.

With a sigh, I drag myself out of bed to get this day started. It's still early, but there's always work waiting. And coffee—at least there's that.

"Good morning, darlin'."

I stop dead in my tracks at the sight of Brooks in my kitchen with a dimpled smile on his face, spatula in hand, and an apron wrapped around his waist.

"What are you doing?" It's a dumb question—the answer's obvious—but I can't quite believe what I'm seeing.

"Cooking you breakfast." He chuckles, the deep rumble of his laugh relaxed and soothing.

My stomach flutters and not from hunger. "You're cooking for me?"

Another laugh has my flutters turning to outright somersaults. "Well, I was trying for a big breakfast, but I burned the first attempt. Now it's just scrambled eggs."

"You didn't throw out the bacon, did you?"

He steps back, revealing a plate of crispy goodness. "Now why would I do that when it's your favorite?"

My mouth waters. Literally waters. But is it because of the yummy food or the delectable man serving it up? Maybe both.

"How'd you know?" I gush, pinching past him to dig into the pile of charred grease, and I barely hold back a moan when the first bite of salt hits my tongue.

Large, rough hands grip the counter on either side of me, boxing me in and sending a ripple of desire coursing through me. His breath is hot at my ear when he murmurs, "I've learned a lot about you, my little darlin' wife. In case you haven't noticed, I invest a lot of time in watching you."

My heart gallops hard in my chest, and I move to capture his lips with my own. The feel of his mouth on mine is more gratifying than ten plates of bacon, but it doesn't last.

After barely a peck, he pulls away, turning his attention back to the eggs.

"Eat up," he encourages, waving the spatula toward my plate. "I've got plans for you today."

"Oh yeah?" The bacon becomes my sole focus as I pretend to be unaffected by his brush-off. "We finally going to get moving on those solar fences?"

When he doesn't answer, I peek up and catch him staring at me intently, the corner of his mouth quirked in a grin.

"What?" I wipe self-consciously at my face and then look down at the front of my shirt to make sure I'm not wearing too much of my breakfast.

"Nothing." He shakes his head with a wide smile. "Just eat."

After breakfast, Brooks leads me to the stables where Hank's waiting with our saddled horses.

"Does everyone know about our plans for today but me? And where exactly are we going?"

The muscles of his spectacular backside bunch and ripple as he mounts his horse. "No more questions. Just follow me."

With a smile, I shut my mouth and follow his lead.

The sun is starting to peek over the small mountain range to the east, casting a warm glow over the shadow of the valley. I love this time of day, when stillness is broken only by the vibrant hum of life waking all around.

It's an energized feeling coffee alone can't produce.

My mare, Tink, blows a loud breath, rolling her head toward Brooks's horse, Ace, as though asking if he's as bored with our slow walk as she is. Ace flicks his mane, nodding in return.

"I think they're anxious to let loose." He looks to me with a sly smile. "What do you say? Race to the east pasture?"

A smile cracks my lips, and a fire stokes in my belly, his

challenge lighting me up, but I don't pause to answer. I grip the horn of my saddle and with a soft nudge of my heels, let Tink know it's time to break free.

No need to tell her twice, she takes off like lightning.

The wind whips my hair, and I let out a loud whoop of excitement, encouraging Tink to pick up the pace. But even at an all-out run, Brooks and Ace whiz past us with ease.

Win or not, racing my horse at breakneck speed fills me with such vast joy, it brings tears to my eyes. It's one of the greatest feelings on earth. The feeling of being alive and free. A feeling given to me by the one and only Brooks Kincaide.

Breathless, I slow Tink to a trot as we reach the east pasture where Brooks waits, murmuring to his horse as he strokes a hand over his shining mane.

"I almost lost my hat," he calls out with a laugh.

"You were flying," I agree, coming up alongside him. "Thanks for that."

"For what? The race?" His brows pinch.

"Yes, and for not forcing your horse to slow so you could let me win."

As though amazed, he shakes his head, a smile still plastered to his handsome face. "You're a fucking delight, Addie Monroe."

"That's Addie Monroe-Kincaide, thank you very much."

A flash of something hot and wild strikes his gaze, sparking a new surge of excitement within me. "I've got something I want to show you."

"Oh yeah?" My dirty mind goes into overdrive.

"It's not what you're thinking," he says through a laugh

and dismounts his horse. "Come on darlin', I think you'll like this."

My curiosity bubbles as I hop down from Tink and follow Brooks to the fence.

We don't go far, and I see it before he says a word. With a loud gasp, I stop short, my feet rooted in place.

Brooks turns with a worried look, and Tink nudges up behind me.

"You…I…is that?" My heart skips out of control.

The apprehension melts from his features, the corners of his mouth tipping back up to a grin that makes him look almost shy.

Now there's a first.

Who knew Brooks Kincaide could be anything other than bold and secure?

Not waiting for his reply, my feet come unglued, and I quickly hand off Tink's reins to him before rushing toward the end of the fence and the single, glorious solar panel, tilted up to the sky.

"You did this?" I ask, still not quite believing it's true.

"Yes. I borrowed a couple of hands from Canyon Spring Ranch to help me set it up." He comes to stand beside me, both horses still in tow. "Obviously, this is just the first step, but I wanted you to see it. For you to know how serious I am about our partnership."

His arm brushes mine, and he leans in closer to whisper, "How serious I am about you."

Blinding emotion tugs me toward him, and grasping his face in both hands, I rise on my toes to kiss him. Hard.

The sound of his groan is pure torture. A sound that spurs me on even more.

We kiss like nothing else matters. Lips pressing. Tongues caressing. Lost in the moment, together.

Until a heavy gust of horse breath washes over us. Ace bumps his big head into Brooks, letting him know just how unhappy he is to be ignored.

Brooks's low laugh rumbles across my lips, and he reluctantly pulls away.

"I think someone's a little jealous," I tease.

"Can't say I blame him." He laughs, brushing a hand across the horse's soft muzzle. "Sorry, buddy, but you'll have to find your own woman."

We spend the next few hours on horseback, surveying the land and discussing the setup for the rest of the solar fence. It's exciting to not only see our project getting off the ground but to believe my dream for this ranch is finally coming true.

To believe the man I married is not only true to his word but to me. That he might be good for me. We might be good for each other.

By the time we reach the pond, the sun is high in the sky and I'm a hot mess. The temperature has risen by at least twenty degrees. I stripped off my long sleeves over an hour ago, leaving me in nothing but my tank and bra, and I can feel the sun baking the skin of my bare shoulders.

I wipe the light sweat from my brow. "We should head back."

"I've got a better idea," Brooks says, urging Ace toward the pond and the small cluster of trees that surrounds it.

I follow him into the shade where we dismount and give the horses time to drink before relieving them of the saddles and letting them free to graze. They'll come when called, especially with the promise of the sugar cubes I've got stored in my satchel.

With the horses off doing their own thing, Brooks turns to me with a soft smile and links his fingers with mine.

"I shouldn't have kept you out in the sun so long," he murmurs, running a finger over my shoulder.

"I'll be fine. But I wouldn't mind taking a dip in the pond."

"That could be nice." He looks around, as though weighing an important decision.

"What?"

"Just looking to see how exposed we are to prying eyes out here."

"Prying eyes?" I laugh at the thought of spies lurking around the fence posts, trying to hide in the open fields.

He gazes at me, hungrily. "Wouldn't want anyone to see my wife in all her naked glory."

My breath catches as his hands run up my sides, bringing my shirt along with them. Slowly, he strips me of my tank, then moves to unclasp my bra.

I help, pulling the straps from my shoulders, then tossing the whole thing aside.

"I've been dreaming about seeing you like this again," he groans, drinking me in.

I tug at his belt, needing to get him naked with me. I'm ready, willing, and oh-so-fucking able to have him right here. Right now.

Suddenly he seems as eager as I am. He pushes my hands out of the way, releasing his belt buckle before pulling his T-shirt over his head and knocking his hat to the ground in the process.

A man's bare chest has never been so enticing. I'm stuck staring at the hard expanse of golden, muscled perfection while he works his fly and toes off his boots at the same time.

"You joining me?" he asks with a turned-on smirk as he drops his pants to the ground, giving me the most glorious show of all time.

Holy fucking hell.

Brooks is...hung. Like a goddamn horse.

I feel like a fiend for even thinking it, but there's simply no other comparison. His cock juts out from a light dusting of hair—thick, long, and hard as granite.

He stands proudly, allowing me a moment to ogle him. And ogle him I do. I think I might be drooling.

"Well?" he urges when I only stand and stare.

With shaking hands, I rush to disrobe, my skin tingling from the feel of his eyes tracking my every move.

He doesn't wait. The minute I'm free of my clothes, he picks me up and carries me into the cool water.

It flows around us, like a refreshing balm to my scorched skin. But even the chill of the water can't douse the heat of desire simmering between us.

He kisses me, his mouth hungry, and his hands roam over my body, caressing and kneading my flesh. Touching me in all the right places.

"Please," I cry, wrapping my legs around his waist,

shamelessly rubbing the crown of his cock through my wet folds. "Fuck me, Brooks, please."

"Don't worry, darlin'," he rasps. "I won't make you beg."

He grunts, and with one smooth stroke, pushes his way inside me.

15

BROOKS

*H*ead back, soft tits against my chest, and golden hair spilling into the water, Addie is naked in my arms. Right where I want her. My rock-hard cock pushes into her. All. The. Way.

Fucking hell.

She whimpers, mouth opening, eyes closing, and I still, letting her adjust to the length and girth of me. Steadying my legs, I force long, slow breaths into my lungs, trying not to come before we even get started. She's so fucking tight, so wet, and it has nothing to do with the water.

When I suggested a ride, this wasn't what I had in mind. But I can't regret this. With Addie, I'd take this kind of ride any day.

"Darlin', you on the pill?" Now isn't the smartest time to ask—pulling out because of a lack of protection will kill me, but I'll do it if needed.

"What?" Eyes dazed and cheeks flushed, she looks at me as if I'm speaking in tongues.

Her long, toned legs wind tighter around my waist and her heated core rubs against me. *Jesus.*

"I don't have a condom," I grit through a locked jaw. "But I've been tested. Do we need to worry about protection?"

I had not planned on fucking her senseless out in the open like this. Fuck, no. This past week was worse than living in hell. As Addie and I spent more time together, preparing for the gala, we were getting closer, but things were also getting harder. Painfully harder.

It was utter torture trying to stick to her rules of engagement. No matter what I did, cold showers or beating off, nothing gave me the release I so desperately craved. Nothing would do but Addie. And forget about the challenges of hiding my perpetual hard-on. What an embarrassing bitch.

Addie is always on my mind, making it difficult to concentrate or get anything done. Her pull, this pull of attraction between us, is so intense I physically ache. When she's near, I can barely keep my hands off her.

"Brooks." Addie climbs me, legs grappling to get higher on my hips. "I'm good. On the pill. Now, fuck me."

She winds her arms around my neck, fingers threading through the ends of my hair.

"Darlin', I've got you." My fingers dig into her luscious ass. "Hang on."

One hand grabs the side of her face, and I mash my mouth over hers, needing to taste her sweetness as I move, driving in and out of her.

Addie whimpers softly, and I stroke my tongue against

hers, taking what is mine. The kiss is hot, wet, and rough like our joined bodies and she meets me thrust for thrust.

Her grasp at the nape of my neck slips and fingernails drag down to my shoulders, piercing skin, as her heels drill into my ass. My mouth feasts on her slick flesh, trekking downward from her jaw, setting a frenzied but attentive pace.

I'm listening to her sounds, feeling the subtle shifts in her body as pleasure and desire ride through her.

She's driving me wild, and I want nothing more than to make her orgasm but not until I say when. My teeth sink into the side of her neck, and she gasps, a growl slipping past her red, swollen lips.

"We come together." My gaze locks onto her wild green eyes, and she mumbles something incoherent.

At the slight turn of my hips, her eyes roll back into her head, and the way she grips me causes my balls to tighten. Her touch, the feel of her hot pussy squeezing me makes my head spin and legs weak.

"Harder," Addie cries, her tits slapping against the water.

Another change to the angle and I swivel my hips hard and fast like the little lady asks. I smash my lips together and try to hold on a little bit more. She feels so fucking good, and I don't want this to end.

I'm there but I need her here with me, both of us free falling together. It doesn't take long until all her muscles coil and tighten. My girl is ready to detonate, and she bites into her bottom lip, clenching her sex around me. I see stars.

"Jesus, Addie, you're fucking perfection." White hot heat burns its way down my spine and straight to my cock. "Come for me, darlin'."

She clings to me, breath ragged, body taut. Blood pounds in my ears, and all I see and feel is her, milking me, losing herself in me. Addie comes hard, hands clutching my head and bringing my face to the crook of her neck.

"Brooks," she screams, giving me all of her.

With one final thrust, I spill into her, shouting her name. Every muscle in my body turns to liquid, and the cool air against the heat of my flesh makes me shiver.

Thank fuck for the water. Legs like jelly, I hold her tight and bend my knees until only our heads are above the surface.

"Brooks, that was amazing." Her voice is breathy, and I brush a wet curl from her cheek, smiling.

"You're amazing." My mouth crashes onto hers, needing another taste and knowing I'll never get enough of her.

***

"*Y*ou've got to be fucking kidding me." My fingers curl around the phone in frustration.

The woman from Geyser Water Technologies sputters, tripping over her third or fourth apology in the same sentence. None of this is her fault, and I sigh, cutting her off to put her out of her misery.

"Look, Frannie. What's done is done." I grind my teeth, holding back a string of curse words. I've subjected the poor woman to my filthy mouth enough already. "The order cancellation is going to set us back easily a few weeks, if not more."

"I really am sorry, Mr. Kincaide. Like I said, the order was

only just canceled yesterday. I can put it through again—"
Frannie's still spinning.

"Yes, do that." I need off this merry-go-round.

I stare down at my gleaming cowboy boots, freshly shined for tonight's gala, and a crazy laugh jumps from my throat. Addie and I are hosting the launch of Greener Prospects to the entire town.

What a fucking joke. How are we going to be successful if we're working against each other? I placed an order for water recycling supplies for the system I plan to install at the Monroe ranch as a surprise for Addie, only to learn she's gone and mucked things up.

"Oh, Mr. Kincaide, is everything all right?" Frannie's voice quakes nervously at my outburst. She must think I'm a lunatic, and right now, I sure as hell feel like one.

"Yes. I'm fine. I apologize for my behavior and mean no disrespect. I'm just surprised...and disappointed."

"Of course, understandably so. Don't you worry now. We'll call you once we have a delivery date."

"All right." I should end the call and finish getting ready for the party, but it turns out I'm a glutton for punishment. Like there isn't already enough salt in my wound, I need to hear her say it one more time. "And you're sure Mrs. Addison Monroe-Kincaide was the one to cancel the order?"

"Uh-huh. I spoke to her myself, and I'm staring at my notes. I always summarize client calls so anybody else can jump right in and pick up where I left off." Her pride at her organizational skills is crystal clear in her voice. Whatever.

"Okay, thank you." I toss the phone onto the bed and hang my head, hands clasping behind my neck.

The need to destroy something burns my insides, or it could be the rage fizzing through my veins. Just when I thought Addie and I were on the same page. We're not only fucking fantastic in bed but in every other way, as well. We were building something, or at least that's what I thought.

Together with George, the two of them were feeling more like a family to me than most of my own. But this—the order cancellation, not bothering to talk to me about it—changes everything.

Was I foolish to think our relationship could be more than a business transaction?

Setting up a small-scale water recycling program at the Monroe ranch was meant to be a good thing. Sure, solar fencing is our first official project. I agreed, and we're moving ahead on it, but I still believed we could do both.

My brilliant idea was to show Addie just how low maintenance and beneficial water recycling could be, and what better way than to have one at her ranch. Give her a chance to see things firsthand.

I even enlisted Hank's help—I'm pretty sure he didn't tell her. He understood it was a surprise and agreed that letting Addie see it in action was the best way to go.

But now the supplies I ordered for the project were canceled by none other than Addie. Why wouldn't she say something to me first instead of putting a stop to it? Where's the partnership and trust in that?

My fingers grip the sides of my head, pulling on my hair as I bellow a string of expletives. The door to my room swings open, and Cole strolls in, thumbs hooked into the waist of his pants.

While oblivious to most things that don't concern him, he has the decency to stop midstride, mouth opening and brows rising to his hairline. "You okay?"

"Hold it right there." Spinning on my heel, I charge him, getting into his face. "You can't just barge in." I glower, nose nearly touching his. "In case you forgot, I'm married. What if Addie had been changing?"

Just the thought of my marriage, of the woman who has taken up residence in not only my mind but also my heart, causes my chest to constrict and lungs to burn.

"But she isn't." He shrugs and walks past me like he owns the place.

I turn, hands curling into my hips in an attempt to not punch the idiot. He drops onto the edge of the bed with a smug grin on his all too pretty face.

"Besides, she's back at her place getting ready for tonight's shindig. She told me so herself. I just came to check on you, see if you needed anything."

"I'm fine. You can leave."

"Yeah, if this is fine." He shakes his head and furrows his brow. "What's got you madder than a bull?"

"Fuck off, Cole, and leave me alone." Storming over to my boots, I shove my feet into them, still fuming about the canceled order and itching to get in Addie's face.

I'm eager to hear why she figured making arbitrary decisions without me is a good idea—a fucking brilliant way to run a partnership.

"Is it Addie?" He stands, straightening his pant leg.

"Not talking to you about this." At the closet door, I rifle through my clothes for the jacket to match the pants I'm wearing.

"Why not? She's about the only thing to rile you up lately. There was a time when Ridge and our parents held the top spot but since the wifey, you're all smiles and shrugs at whatever bullshit they throw your way." He admires his reflection in the mirror, fingers combing through his already perfectly coiffed hair.

I want nothing more than to mess it up, shove him around a bit, and kick him out. But I won't. It's Cole, and while his chatter is annoying, he isn't the object of my ire. He's the one brother I could spend the rest of my life with and be just fine.

"And your fucking point?" I slip on my jacket and grab my hat.

"What did she do now? And why are you putting yourself through this?"

"Through what?" I pause on my way to the door, cocking my head to one side, puzzled.

"I thought this marriage was business."

"It is." I resume my exit from the room with Cole on my heels.

"Then why are you tying yourself up in knots like this? Whatever it is, she can't be worth it."

An explosion of emotions riots inside of me, and I spin to face him, pushing him back into the room and shutting the door. This house is never empty; someone is always listening.

"Stay the fuck out of my marriage. She and I have a few things to settle. Bullshit she thought she'd pull without talking to me first. We'll figure it out." I hate the way the last words sound coming from my mouth. More hopeful than certain.

"Brooks, no woman is worth this much hassle. If she can't be trusted, then walk away. You'll still be part of the ranch, and who knows, in time you could get top spot. Ridge isn't going to meet Pa's demands."

"Yeah, I don't think he will, either, but that's neither here nor there. I made a commitment to Addie…" My gaze darts away from his intense eyes, not able to show him just how deep her latest actions have cut.

Almost as an afterthought—and this shocks me—I clear my throat, straighten my shoulders, and I add, determinedly, "I'm doing what's right for the ranch."

Done with this conversation, I march from the room and out to my truck as fast as possible. I need to talk to Addie.

The gala is in the Majestic Ballroom—that's what it's called, although *majestic* is a stretch—of the town's lodge. I toss my keys to the valet we arranged just for this event. For Prospect, it's a luxury most would scoff at, but it's a nice touch. Besides, in this case, the valet are two teenagers in their best jeans and button-down shirts. I give the one closest to me, a boy who looks barely driving age, a stern *don't get a scratch on my truck* look and hurry into the building.

I chuckle under my breath. We're hosting an environmental event and yet, most of the guests drive gas guzzlers. I suppose we have to start somewhere.

Locating our party is easy. As I near the room's entrance, chatter and music filter into the hallway, and inside is packed.

My chest swells with pride, battling to overshadow or

squash my still very alive anger. Almost the entire town is here. Ranchers, local business owners, and busybodies mingle, eating, drinking, and laughing.

This is good.

It takes a few minutes of scanning the crowd to find her.

My wife.

She's across the room, looking as beautiful as ever.

Fuck. Why does everything hurt when I look at her?

My first instinct is to find a dark corner, lift up her dress, pull her panties down, and spank her sweet ass.

Ah no.

Then I'd want to fuck her, and right now, there's no time for that. She already got one over on me. She betrayed me, and we're going to have words.

16

ADDISON

emy Harding, a balding man in his mid-fifties who runs one of the two local grocery stores, is chatting my ear off—something about shrimp cocktail and napkins—but I'm having a hard time concentrating on anything other than the burning pit of outrage, brewing deep in my belly.

With the stroke of a magic wand, or more likely the flash of cold hard cash, the lodge ballroom has been transformed from intimate, down-home country to upscale, stuffy professional. There's an overflowing table of food to my right, champagne flowing from an actual goddamn fountain to my left, and the evidence of my stupidity is posted all over the room.

I never thought myself gullible, but it seems all it took to manipulate me was a big dick. A big dick who really knows how to use his big dick...

Too bad getting screwed doesn't feel quite as magical this time around.

"Reminds me of a joke," Remy booms, jerking my attention back to him and this farce of an event.

I force a polite smile his way, even though all I really want to do is scream.

"Tell me if you've heard this one." He launches into what I can tell is sure to be a groaner, and I feign interest while doing another visual sweep of the packed room.

It looks like everyone is here—the entire town of Prospect, dressed in their Sunday best. Even Sage is in attendance, looking posh as always, and dragging Ridge and Trey along with her. Scarlett, Jett, and Cole are here as well, scattered amongst the other guests.

Only two important people are missing tonight. Daddy, who would be here if I'd let him, but I could tell wasn't feeling up to it, and Brooks.

Of course, Brooks is the one person who really counts. He's the one who should be by my side, tonight of all nights. The one who should protect his junk when he finally shows up, because boy-oh-fucking-boy is he on my shit list.

"Addie!" Hannah interrupts Remy mid corny joke. "I've been looking all over for you! Mr. Harding, do you mind if I steal her for a minute? My husband has something important he needs to tell her."

Remy turns a deep shade of crimson, his eyes flicking to Hannah's movie star husband, Parker, and nods. "Not at all."

Thank goodness for the distraction of my best friend and her famous husband.

She sweeps me far away from the buffet table, where we're less likely to be overheard by the town gossip mill.

"What the hell is going on?" she whispers, keeping her bright smile in place.

A shaky breath passes my lips, and I try not to break down in a fit of angry tears. "I don't know. But I swear when I find him, I'm going to…"

The ramp-up to my tirade fades when I notice Brooks stalking toward us from across the room.

He's dressed in a designer suit and tie, his white shirt crisp against his golden skin. With his hair tamed, face cleanly shaved, and a scowl etched on his handsome features, he looks like a man in charge. A ranching god.

The future boss of Canyon Spring Ranch.

My insides melt at the sight of his dark expression, which makes him seem even more formidable. More desirable. More enticing.

My body's response to him is immediate, but no matter how hot or needy he makes me, I will not fall for any of his charming lies. I won't let him make me an even bigger fool than he has already.

He stops abruptly in front of us with his shoulders bunched and hands curled to angry fists.

Clearly agitated, he turns to Hannah with a sharp nod. "Hello, Hannah. Nice to see you." His rough voice betrays his courteous words.

She doesn't bother acknowledging him and instead takes my hand in hers. "I'll be right over there with Parker if you need me. We're both here for you."

"Thank you. You're the best."

The acid in my stomach rolls uncomfortably, and I avoid Brooks's gaze, choosing to watch Hannah glide toward her adoring husband, who nestles her to his side—their love for one another seeming to spill from every pore.

Did Brooks and I ever stand a chance at happiness like that?

"Addie." There's an edge of warning in his low voice. "I don't want a scene in front of all these people, but I gotta know what the hell you were thinking."

"Pardon me?" Fire leaps up my throat and I turn on him, not bothering to hide the storm brewing inside me.

"You heard me, darlin'."

"Don't you darlin' me, Brooks Kincaide. You've got a lot of nerve, coming at me with any kind of complaint right now."

"Complaint?" He leans closer, his heat cascading over me. "Is that what you call it when the person you trusted most goes behind your back?"

His words hit hard, bruising my already tender heart and throwing me into a spiral of confusion and doubt. His eyes are narrowed, and lips pinched with a look of frustration, maybe even anger. But I'm the one who's been betrayed.

What kind of mind game is he playing?

"I don't know, Brooks. You tell me. When you were scheming with your family on how to best stick it to the Monroes, did you think I'd only have complaints? Did you not think I'd take action?"

"What the hell are you talking about?" He darts a glance around the room to see who might be watching and stands a little taller, fussing with his tie.

Right now, I'd like to choke him with it—audience or not.

"You're the one who canceled my supply order with Geyser Technologies." His jaw hardens when his harsh gaze lands back on mine. "Why, Addie?"

What the ever loving... "I have no idea what you're talking about."

"Don't lie to me. Are you so intent on having your own way you'd sabotage our partnership?"

"What partnership?" I growl, my nails digging into my palms. "We don't have one. At least, not according to the signs."

His mouth opens in protest, but he only stands stupefied, staring at me like he doesn't recognize me. And maybe he doesn't. Maybe he never knew me at all.

I certainly don't know him as well as I thought.

"There's nothing you can say or do that will make up for this, Brooks." I point to the giant blue banner strung across the front of the room.

The banner which prominently displays our brand-new company logo and the Kincaide family name. No note of Monroe anywhere in this room—not on a single sign or promotional pamphlet.

He didn't just put his family name first, he left mine out completely.

Left *me* out.

His eyes grow wide when he looks up to the banner, as though he's seeing this for the first time.

"What kind of fucking partnership is that?" My face feels hot, and my throat raw.

"Addie," he whispers. "I swear, I didn't do this. I didn't know."

"Save it." I hold up a hand, stopping his denial. "All you've ever cared about is your ranch and your family's ridiculous power play. I knew it, yet still hoped you might come to care about something more." *I thought you might care about me.* "But I was wrong."

"I care. Hell, I sunk my own money into the order you canceled. Because. I. Care. This—" He gestures to the banner. "—this is just a misunderstanding."

"No, Brooks." I shake my head, willing myself not to cry.

I can't believe he's going to keep carrying out this lie. To try and gaslight me into believing any of this is my fault. How did I not see this side of him before?

"We had a deal. This is more than a misunderstanding. It's a breach of contract."

"So, that's all our marriage is to you? A business deal?"

"Of course." I push my shoulders back, not allowing my body to slump or sway, despite the effort it's taking to stay upright. "It's what we agreed to."

"What about the time we spent together, getting to know each other? Sharing parts of myself I've never shared with anyone? The best sex of my life? You're telling me none of that was real? It was all just part of our agreement?"

"The only thing real about our marriage is the certificate." My heart squeezes a pathetic, fractured beat, resisting the lie. "You and I both knew it going in. We agreed to no feelings, remember? It's all fake."

"Fake." His voice is wooden, and he glares at me, mashing his lips into a tight line.

"Yes. Fake," I repeat, bashing the point home, not for his sake but my own.

"Brooks! Addison!" Sage calls to us with melodramatic flare, and Brooks's head snaps to her attention. "Have you met Congressman Landry?"

She's standing close to a tall, willowy man whose smile reminds me of a shark, both of them watching us expectantly.

Brooks raises his hand, indicating we need a moment.

"Tell her I'm not feeling well." I back away from the scene. "Hell, tell her whatever you want. You're good at making shit up."

"Addie, please." He stalks forward, his eyes begging me to stay, but I don't stop my retreat. I can't. I refuse to let this man, or anyone, break me.

Never again.

But he halts my shuffling steps with a strong grip around my arm. "We need to talk about this."

"Hey, you two," Ridge interrupts, slapping Brooks on the back and tossing me a cocky wink. "Your lovers' quarrel will have to wait. Mama wants to see you."

Brooks's cinch around my arm loosens, allowing me to pull free, and I take a single step back, secretly hoping he'll follow.

But he doesn't.

He runs both hands over his front, smoothing his tie yet again, and nods to Ridge with a forced smile. "We'll be there in a minute."

"No," Ridge says through a sarcastic chuckle. "She wants you now."

I continue to back slowly away, staring at my husband, my head shaking in hurt disbelief.

Still, he doesn't try to stop me. Instead, he drops his head like a cowed dog and allows Ridge to drag him away.

At least it's clear where his loyalty lies—but I guess I should have already known. Daddy was right all along. A Kincaide can't be trusted.

Not even when you are one.

I turn in search of Hannah, blocking out the string of *I told you so*'s running through my head. I need to get the hell out of here.

Or maybe drown myself in the fountain of champagne.

But instead of Hannah, my gaze collides with Derek's. He's watching me from mere feet away, with a nasty smile glued to his face—gratified by my clash with Brooks. Go figure, my jilted ex had a front row ticket to the show.

Why the fuck is he even here?

With my head held high, I ignore his taunting leer and angle my way across the room, giving a half-hearted wave to Sheriff Gilbert as I pass. Why is he always around whenever I'm in the mood to punch someone?

After too many forced smiles and strained hellos, I finally spot Hannah. She's too short to actually see with the crowd around her, but Parker's gleaming smile stands out for miles.

"Excuse me," I mumble, pushing my way past the star-struck gawkers, and receive an elbow to the left boob for my efforts.

Can this night seriously get any worse?

"Folks. Folks," Parker calls to his mini-throng of admirers. "It's been a pleasure, but if you don't mind, we're here tonight for our friend Addison Monroe-Kincaide, to help her celebrate her fantastic new green venture."

The small crowd grumbles but gives their half-hearted applause before starting to finally disperse.

"Please consider contributing to Greener Prospects," Parker appeals as they retreat.

He'd have made a great spokesperson for our business. Too bad I didn't think to ask him before the whole thing imploded.

"You okay?" Hannah hands me a glass of bubbly.

"Not really." I gulp back the sparkling liquid. "I'm going to need a stronger drink. Or six."

I sneak another look around the room to see how many eyes are on us.

Thankfully, most of the guests are either busy loading plates with free gourmet food or are indulging Brooks's preening mother and her congressman guest. Even Derek has vanished amongst the crowd, and I breathe a little easier.

"Can I ask you guys for the biggest favor ever? Mostly you, Parker."

"Are you kidding? You know we'd do anything for you." Hannah hooks her arm with mine.

"Is it illegal?" Parker winces.

"Well, I'll do anything for you," Hannah says with a smile, nudging her husband in the side. "And since Parker will do anything for me, it's basically the same thing. Illegal or not."

"Don't worry, I just need you to do what you do best, Parker. Act your heart out."

He gives me a quizzical look.

"I need to get out of here, and I want you to cover for me."

"If that's what you really want," Parker agrees, rubbing at the back of his neck. "But I have to ask...why?"

My eyes bug and I raise my hand to the ceiling where the stupid damn banner hangs over us—over me—like a neon sign, advertising my broken trust. "Isn't that reason enough?"

But is it enough? And is it truly the reason I'm leaving?

Hannah bites her lip and Parker nods. "It's a blow," he agrees. "But Greener Prospects is your baby, and it seems a shame to abandon it over something like this."

"I'm not," I argue, struggling to catch my breath around this choking sensation. "I'd never surrender my dream."

But I will run out on it for a moment if it means protecting my pride.

Or am I running to protect my heart?

"Parker might be way off-script," Hannah says with a soft smile, "but he has a point. Are you going to let them drive you away from your own party?"

"Yes." My chin trembles. "And I have to go now, before it's too late."

My marriage, the partnership, Brooks's devotion—it may all be counterfeit, but I can't deny this bruising ache in my chest is real.

It's already too late, I realize. There's nothing fake about this feeling.

I'm in love with my husband.

17

BROOKS

My face aches, my head pounds, and all my muscles are tight and brittle from the endless fake smiles and even phonier laughs at tonight's party. I'm a fraud.

And damn, my chest. It feels like the life has been squeezed out of it—and it was.

Every ounce of joy perished when Addison stormed out of our own launch party. *Thanks for the support, darlin'.*

Yeah, that pretty much sums up my night.

Although, even without her there, the Monroe name and the mention of Addie did bring in its fair share of potential business and local ranchers who want in on our venture. All ranchers interested were easily swayed by the tax saving implications and that Greener Prospects would do the heavy lifting. We'd negotiate the initial contracts and pricing, as well as provide oversight and work out the kinks during installation and implementation on each of the ranches.

The night is as black as a raven's feather, and there's a nip in the air even for June with the temperature dipping to the low forties. I follow the taillights of Mama's truck up the dark and dusty driveway to our home.

Canyon Spring Ranch.

Are the constant battles and heartache worth it? I want so badly to run this ranch, but at what cost?

The cattle, horses, and the very earth of this place are in my blood. My earliest memory of my life is about the ranch, and every beat of my heart belongs to this land.

Fuck. But Addie.

She has quickly become a contender for top spot in my heart and mind—and before tonight, I might have said she was leading.

Aw, screw it. Who am I kidding? Our marriage is just a business transaction to her. She said so herself.

The ranch is all I have and all I need.

But I'm done playing by Mama's rules and letting Ridge's threats get to me.

Those assholes were behind changing all the banners at tonight's party. They were the ones to remove the Monroe name from every scrap of promotional material.

They didn't have to tell me. I saw the underhanded bullshit in their eyes. In the way Mama accepted all the praise, and Ridge gloated to the congressman as if this venture was the family's idea. The fucker even hinted the whole thing had been his baby, but he could only take it so far.

When Landry pressed for more details, I was the one to save Ridge's ass and answer Landry's questions. I was the one to secure the statesman's endorsement, and I wish Addie had been there. She'd have shined.

The truck now parked, I sit and watch Ridge bound from the vehicle beside me toward the front door, hat in hand. Mama takes her sweet time, prancing up the walkway with Trey at her side. She hasn't a care in the world.

Well, I'm about to change that.

I jump from the truck, slamming the door just loud enough to give the two of them pause, and I use the jarring moment to march ahead of them.

With the door in hand, I gesture for them to enter the house, and Trey studies me warily. Mama proffers a gracious smile. The four of us are inside the foyer—Ridge with one foot on the bottom step of the staircase—when I clear my throat.

"Tonight is the last time any of you interfere with Greener Prospects." I point from Mama to Ridge, while Trey frowns, confused and vexed. "The Kincaide name is one half of this partnership. It's fifty-fifty and neither of you had any right to change those promotional materials. The Monroes are here to stay."

I hope what I'm saying is true and even if Addie and I are done, we can still make a go at this business venture.

Ridge releases a bitter chuckle, his gaze admonishing. "Brooks, when are you going to learn to be a businessman? We don't need the Monroes, so why are you even bothering with Addie?"

"Because she's my wife," I bellow, getting in his face.

The heat of my anger surges up the back of my neck, and my thundering heartbeat is all I hear. My brother's shocked at my conviction, taking another step up the stairs, away from me.

Trey is now at my side, cautiously wrapping an arm around my bicep in a firm but moderate grip. "Easy. Settle down."

"Both of you are right. We don't need the Monroes, but Addison is Brooks's wife, and this venture is a partnership and will be billed as such going forward." With my mother's decree, she feigns fatigue, covering her hand over her mouth to stifle a yawn as she nods to Trey to let me go.

"Good night, Brooks. Tonight was a success. Well done." Her long gown swishes as she steps around me to take the stairs.

Ridge stomps upstairs without a word, and for once, while not placated with my mother's comment, I take some satisfaction in leaving my brother speechless. He always likes to have the last word.

"We're not done." I stare intently at my mother, and my tone leaves no room for argument.

Her spine stiffens with a noticeable rattle to her body, as if jolted by a cattle prod. Narrowing her icy gaze, she steps closer to me. "Yes, we are. I'm exhausted, and what's done is done. You have my word it won't happen again."

Unable to hold back my contempt, I scoff, and she straightens as if trying to make herself taller, and her tone turns frosty. "Count this evening as a win, Brooks."

With her veiled threat delivered—the *or else* is implied— she deflates, rubbing at her temple with a sigh. I'm a nuisance she can't be bothered with, and isn't this how it's always been? Well, not tonight.

"I'm not asking you. I'm telling you we are going to talk. It's time to discuss Pa's will."

Trey clears his throat uncomfortably, sliding around me to the spot just vacated by our mother at the bottom of the stairs. "Well, if you'll excuse me, I'm going to bed."

I'm surprised at his desire to make a quick exit. Normally, he's Mama's pit bull and would be telling me to knock it off. But now, he doesn't even look her way. In fact, he makes quick work of disappearing, taking the stairs two at a time.

"What is it?" She crosses her arms over her chest and glares at me, not in the least bit tolerant or amused.

"I've fulfilled Pa's requirements of the will well before Ridge, and I'm already proving I can do this." I plant my hands on my waist, feeling the need to make a larger presence. "What's Ridge done since Pa died except skirt around the idea of a wife and give orders? I've launched a sustainability partnership that's not only benefited the ranch for today but for future generations. Not to mention what it's done for the town and for community relations. And if you need to hear what else I've done, let's talk about what I do day in and day out for the ranch—"

"Enough." She holds up her hand, and her mouth twists into an ugly, prickly shape, something like gnarly barbed wire.

"You may not want to face it, but Pa was wrong. I am the right person to head Canyon Spring Ranch. My track record proves it, and I'm tired of having to jump through hoops every time you decide you want to cause me more grief or kick me down a notch or two." My voice rises higher and higher with each word, needing her to understand I am serious.

"I'm not going to take your bullshit anymore. I'm done with the stunts like the one you pulled tonight." My finger pokes at my chest and I pull my shoulders back. "I am the head of Canyon Spring."

"Just who the hell do you think you're talking to?" She's meaner than a bull with her nostrils flaring and eyes pointed. "Brooks, you will never be the head of this ranch, you got that?"

Her words are a punch to the gut, and I don't know why. It isn't something that has been said before, but this time is different. Maybe it's because I finally hear her, and the meaning sinks in.

Or maybe is it because Pa isn't here to appeal to? Not that he'd cave, but at least I'd buy myself more time. I'd give them something to stew over while I worked my ass off proving them wrong. Then things would settle back into the way they were.

Or maybe it's the strange, maniacal way she's staring at me. No, *through* me. Inhumane and cold.

"I am the head of Canyon Spring Ranch," I repeat, digging deep for the same, if not more, confidence than before.

She releases a *pfft,* crinkling her nose as if she smells shit. "You're too much of a softy. When we had to cut from the staff, you wasted four weeks trying to find other jobs for the workers, either here at the ranch or somewhere else in town. That's commendable and all, but it isn't a smart business decision. I need someone who will be ruthless."

"And you think that's Ridge?" My chest constricts, feeling the loss but not willing to give up. "He wants the glory, but he isn't willing to do the work."

"That may be so, but that's for me to deal with now, isn't it? Brooks, this is your problem." She's cold and impenetrable as stone, glowering at me. "Every time you were told to do something you didn't want to do, you had to be cajoled or coaxed into it. I can't have that. I don't have the time, energy, or patience for it. For you."

"And there's nothing I can do to change your mind?" I hate the way I sound.

The silly little boy I once was, the one who just never measured up, rears his head. He's curling up inside my chest with the unending ache to be seen, to be chosen.

"No." She stomps toward the stairs.

The loss of this evening, everything I've ever wanted—Addie, the ranch—they're gone. My marriage is a fucking joke.

Addison Monroe, the one thing I never knew I wanted. And I fucking had her. It was glorious and perfect and...shit, I had her for what? A second.

I want her back, but she's made it clear I'm not worth fighting for.

And the ranch—well, it was never mine to begin with.

So where does that leave me? I don't have a fucking clue, but one thing is for sure, I can't go on like this. If I continue the way I have for most of my life, I'll lose anything I have left of myself.

"And what if I walk away from the ranch?" My voice booms up at my mother now halfway up the staircase. "Wash my hands of everything and step down as Ridge's right-hand man?"

The questions are like broken glass, jagged and biting in my throat, and as much as it hurts, it's my last move. The only move I have if I want to make sure I come out of this as some sort of human, even if I'm broken and in pieces.

Mama slowly turns, peering at me over her shoulder with a wicked sneer. "Well, that's your choice to make." Shadowed by the night, her face looks almost ghoulish like some devil creature. How fitting.

"Is it? 'Cause it feels more like you're pushing me out. Not just now, but my whole damn life...I just don't understand why. Why am I not good enough, Mama?"

"Because you're not my son." Her voice is devoid of emotion, and she stares at me blankly. "I never intended on telling you—your father didn't want me to...but I guess he no longer has a say, does he?"

I blink, shifting my weight from foot to foot, unsure I heard her correctly. The house is still—nothing is moving, not even air.

A fierce revulsion claws up my throat and burns my stomach. "What? You really think I'm stupid, don't you?" My laughter is violent and bitter. "This reeks of desperation, especially for you, Mama. Do I really threaten you that much?"

Still flat, emotionless, she stares past me into the darkness of the house. The family home she now wants me to believe isn't fully mine.

"When we were young, newly married, your father couldn't

keep it in his pants." She twists her face in disgust, the first show of true feeling. "I agreed to keep you, acknowledge you as my own, so long as he took care of things and never strayed again."

"Took care of things?" My heart sinks at what that could mean when it comes to Sage and Devlin Kincaide. So many questions race through my mind. If I'm to believe her, who is my mother? Did they try to get rid of me?

My belly aches and this day, this conversation, is taking its toll. I want to sit down, but I dare not move. I'll never let her see any weakness, especially now when she wants to rip my life apart.

"What the hell does 'take care of things' mean?" Rage rings in my words.

"Before you run off on some quest to find your mommy, don't bother." She leans into the banister of the stairs, and her shrewd gaze never veers from me. "Your mother was some ranch hand's sister. An easy lay and easier to pay off to leave town. She never even tried to keep you and then died in a rodeo accident before your fifth birthday." She delivers hit after hit as if reading a recipe.

I'm numb to this tale, unfeeling to a story that isn't mine. No matter how she wants me to wear this, make it mine and drown in it, I won't.

In this moment, clarity barrels over me like a freight train, and I stumble away from her.

Hate never felt so real as in this moment. For all the dark and wicked things I've wished upon my father, never did I feel true hatred. All I'd ever wanted was his love and approval. Shit, even Sage's...my mother.

But this person in front of me isn't my mother. Thank fuck. And she's another kind of heartless.

We share no blood.

Relief, calm, and understanding wash over me.

She isn't my mother. And none of this changes who I am.

"Brooks, this stays between us and will never go beyond the family. And even at that, I don't want you to share this with anyone. Do you understand me?" She arches a brow and starts tapping the ball of her foot when I'm not quick to respond. "I will not stand for the entire town knowing... knowing about our past."

Something unknown, almost human, and definitely uncomfortable skitters across her perfectly made-up face.

Sage abhors airing our dirty laundry. Only the best and most perfect appearance for the Kincaides.

Is this my chance to beat her at her own game? Make demands and threaten to expose us all, what Devlin Kincaide did to her, in exchange for what I want—Canyon Spring Ranch?

Tempting, but I'd not only be exposing Sage but the entire family. There would be judgement and a definite fall from grace with some of the families, even some of our rivals.

The townspeople don't think we're perfect, but they fear us. If I brought this secret to light, I'd only be giving others the first bullet to put us down.

No. I won't do that.

"You said you wanted a chance to change my mind..." She moves on as if her word won't be challenged and now, she dangles a carrot in front of me. Always the one to want the upper hand.

I nod, not trusting myself to speak. A surge of adrenaline courses through my body, curious to see where this is going. I may still have a place here.

"Well, if you're serious about proving yourself—doing anything to show you can do the job—I want Greener Prospects. We don't need the Monroes. They wouldn't know how to make a profit if a pile of cash was dumped in front of them."

Her fingers curl around the railing, and one corner of her mouth tips up. "You get to run the ranch if you take the reins on Greener Prospects and dump Addie. We don't need to be saddled with the likes of her kind. They're dead weight and an embarrassment."

"You're asking me to break my business contract and my wedding vows?"

"That's what I said."

"And I'm supposed to trust you? Trust that if I deliver, you'll hold up your end of the deal. Give Devlin's bastard child the top spot?" The words rip from my mouth in a growl.

She flinches but quickly composes herself. "Brooks, you're like a son to me despite how you came into this family." Her tone softens and my stomach roils at her obscene lies. If I was like a son, she wouldn't have treated me like an outsider since the moment Pa died.

In fact, the more I think about it, the more I believe it was her influence—her insistence—that lead Pa to name Ridge successor instead of me. My father was a hardass, but even if I believed Ridge was the favorite, Pa wouldn't have so easily bucked tradition and spurned his firstborn. Not when I've worked so damn hard for him.

"I didn't tell you the truth to upset you. I merely thought it was time you knew. Time you understood why your father's will was written the way it was."

"The sins of the father."

Her features twist in confusion. "What?"

My father was a formidable force, yet Sage was able to bend him to her will. I used to think it was their love, but now I see she had him by the balls. She never forgave him for his infidelity, and every day of his sorry life, made him pay for that sin.

Or better yet, made me pay.

Yes, now it's all so easy to see. But now, the tables are turned.

"Nothing." I try but fail to hide a maniacal smile. "I just want to be clear on your offer... If I get rid of Addie, you'll give me control of Canyon Spring Ranch? No other strings?"

"Yes. It's your choice, Brooks. What's more important to you? Addie or this ranch?"

18

ADDISON

"So have you decided what you're going to do?" Hannah asks through a yawn.

I rub my eyes with the back of my hand and move my mug closer to the gurgling coffee maker. "Well, I was going to be polite and wait for the whole pot to brew, but if you're forcing me into this conversation right now, I'm taking the first cup as soon as there's enough."

"Sorry." She shuffles forward, retrieving a mug off the shelf and setting it beside mine. Pretty soon we'll be jockeying for position. "You must be hurting this morning."

"My head's a little sore."

"Mine, too." She bumps me with her shoulder. "But I wasn't really talking about the hangover."

"I know," I sigh. "It's adding to my misery, though."

Despite doing my best to drown my sorrows, last night is still crystal clear. After fleeing the party with Hannah and

Parker in tow, we cracked into my secret stash of Hopper's award-winning moonshine, and it flowed like water between the three of us. That stuff burns like a sonuvabitch going down but was still more tolerable than the sting of Brooks's deceit.

Even now, his betrayal is a fresh brand across my heart. Every time I think about that obnoxious blue banner with the Kincaide name in bold block letters, I relive the humiliation of Brooks's con job displayed for the entire town to see.

"The whole thing just makes me so fucking angry."

"Angry?" She taps her mug and raises an eyebrow at me. "Or hurt?"

I flex my fingers, preparing to sneak closer to the coffee pot. "I don't know...both?"

The brew finally finishes, and I rush to pour us each a cup. I can't wait for the first sip to hit my lips and hardly care that it scalds my tongue in the process.

"You may not want to hear this," Hannah says, after giving me a moment to bask in the glow of caffeine. "But I think you're making a mistake."

"What?" I sputter, slopping coffee down the front of me. "You're giving me this advice now? Why didn't you stop me at the altar when I asked you?"

"Because marrying Brooks isn't the mistake I'm referring to. In fact, I wouldn't call that a mistake at all—I think it was actually a good decision. Bold as hell, but good."

My chest feels suddenly tight, and the contents of my stomach are threatening to make an appearance. "What am I missing here? What other mistake have I possibly made?"

Her shoulders rise and fall on a heavy sigh. "I love you, Addie, but sometimes you're so closed off even I can't figure out what's going on in your head. A relationship needs good communication to work. A lot of it. I don't see you making that effort."

"So, you're saying it's my fault Brooks stabbed me in the back?"

"What? No!" She takes another deep breath, visibly calming herself. "I'm saying you don't even know for sure that he did. You ran out last night like the place was on fire, and you did it at the first hint of trouble."

Her wide eyes implore for my understanding. I know she has a point, but it's still hard to hear my best friend call me out on my fuckups.

The men I've dated in the past are all evidence of how I push people away. When my relationships end, I'm the one cutting the cord. I'm the one running the other direction before things get too serious. Before I can get attached and they can leave me. Hurt me.

But now...shit, now I don't even know where things stand. Are Brooks and I still together? Was last night just a fight or the end of it all?

Maybe he got what he wanted. Maybe the only real thing I'll ever have is regret.

"Listen." She rubs her hand over my arm, begging me with her comforting touch not to withdraw. "I know after your mom left the way she did it's hard for you to trust. But don't you think you owe it to yourself to try?"

"I did try." I pull back from her, crossing my arms over my

chest. "I thought Brooks and I had a real partnership—not just a contract on paper, but an actual bond growing between us. I trusted him. I thought we were building a business *and* a future. But then at the gala, it felt like he was moving to that future without me. Like he'd already left me behind."

"Oh, honey!" She reaches for me again, and even though I'm tempted to retreat, I allow her sympathy. "You really are in love with him, aren't you?"

"Does it matter? After last night, I don't hold much hope of him feeling the same. Maybe I just need to face the reality that this thing was always going to end—he would have left me sooner or later."

She nods, her eyes pooling with unshed tears, but she's wearing an expression that makes me question whether she truly agrees.

A low moan sounds behind us, and Parker stumbles into the kitchen, swiping a hand over his face. "I think someone tried to kill me last night."

Hannah and I both giggle at his dramatic performance, but I catch her wiping under her eyes. I turn to pour her lightweight of a husband some coffee, secretly dabbing at my own tears before they get out of control.

We take turns poking fun at Parker and drink enough coffee to last us 'til midnight, at least. By the time they're ready to leave, it's just rounding noon, and I realize Daddy hasn't come out for his breakfast.

Worry and guilt immediately set in.

"Should we stay and make sure everything's all right?" Hannah asks.

"No, it's fine," I tell her, even though the little voice at the back of my mind is whispering what a terrible daughter I am. "You've got a ranch to run and so do I."

"Okay, well, call me if you need *anything*."

After promising to call and reassuring them everything will be okay, I bolt to the back of the house, toward Daddy's bedroom.

I'm not sure what I'm expecting—the worst-case scenario is too scary to even contemplate—but I'm surprised when all I find is an empty room.

His bedroom door hangs open with no sign of him anywhere. His bed is made, his boots gone from under it, and his bathroom is empty, as well.

"Daddy?" I call loudly, even though I already know he's not here.

I wander through the house, looking for signs of him, wondering where he might have gone. He's probably just out with Hank, but with each corner I turn, with each empty room I face, a foreboding sense of aloneness threatens to overwhelm me.

Is this what my life is destined to become? A desolate void of never-ending loneliness?

What if Brooks doesn't just shut me out of the business, but out of his life? What will happen once my ranch has folded, the workers are gone, Daddy passes, and all I'm left with is this decaying house and my broken dreams?

God, I should have never trusted him in the first place. I should have listened to my father, learned from his experience, kept my barriers up and defenses sharp.

The sound of a vehicle rolling up the driveway catches my attention. I dart to the front door, pushing my way onto the porch, breathless from the exertion and hoping to see Daddy hobbling up the walkway.

But instead, I find Brooks stalking toward me.

"What are you doing here?" I demand, my voice tight and almost panicked sounding.

He stops at the bottom step and pulls his hat lower, shielding his clear blue gaze from the sun and blocking me out in the process. "We need to talk. About last night. About us."

"I think last night spoke for itself, don't you? What more is there to say?"

"Really?" He climbs the porch stairs two at a time, his body moving with a fluid grace that reminds me of the way he danced on our wedding night.

I bite my lip, fighting off feelings of tenderness.

The closer he comes, the higher my heart soars, but I hold my ground, allowing him to get as close as he dares. I refuse to invite him inside, though. It seems safer to keep him out here. Outside of my walls. Outside of my life.

"How about an apology?" He stops just out of reach and crosses his arms over his chest.

"What?" I scoff, heat rising to my cheeks. "You expect me to apologize? Are you really that obtuse?"

"Fuck's sakes!" he barks. "I thought maybe we were both responsible and should share the blame for how things turned out. If you need me to start, then so be it. I'm sorry."

"You're sorry?" My voice isn't much more than a whisper, the air stolen from my lungs.

"Yes." He shifts his stance, leaning just a fraction closer.

There's a challenge clear in his tone. "What's wrong with that?"

"It's not enough!" I yell, gritting my teeth against the useless, prickling sensation of unwanted tears. I will not cry. *I will not fucking cry*.

"Feeling regretful, admitting when you're wrong, saying you're sorry—it's important to me, Addison. I thought it'd be important to you, too."

Addison.

Not darlin' or even just Addie. He says my full name like it's a curse, condemning me for wanting more than mere words can provide.

"It's. Not. Enough," I repeat, digging my heels in. Maybe I'm being too stubborn, but this is my metaphorical line in the sand.

"Well, what fucking more do you want?"

"It's too late," I whisper, holding back a sob. "Our deal is already broken. You can't give me what I want."

He shakes his head, the exasperation clear in his expression. "I thought I could do right by you, I really did. Fuck, I thought I could do right by everyone and once...maybe just once get what I wanted too. But now I realize how impossible that is."

The air around me seems to thicken, making it hard to breathe. This is it, the moment I've been dreading. The moment he chooses to walk away. The moment he tells me we're through.

"I guess neither of us got what we bargained on," I say flatly. The walls around my heart are cracked and crumbling, but I don't let it show. "Guess it's a good thing this deal was only temporary."

"Is that how you always saw it?" His voice breaks. "You never once thought it could be more? Never once thought *we* could be more?"

It would be so easy to run to him right now. To throw my arms around his wide shoulders, kiss his delectable mouth, and beg him to love me. Beg him to never leave.

But what would that get me? Another day, week, or maybe if I'm lucky a couple more months? And then what?

I'll be left with nothing but deeper misery when he finally decides to walk away for good. Because he will. It's inevitable, isn't it?

"It doesn't matter what I thought. It's over."

"Fuck this." His hand slashes through the air, punctuating his anger. "I never stood a chance with you. I don't know why I even bothered to fucking try."

He turns from me, stomping back toward the stairs. But at the last minute, he spins back around, hitting me with a fierce glare. "I'd have sacrificed anything for you, Addie. Fuck...I'd sacrifice it all if you'd just fucking let me."

When he speeds away in his truck, spewing gravel in all directions, he leaves me with tears coursing down my cheeks and rage burning deep in my belly.

How dare he put this back on me—blame me—when he was the one who shattered my trust and stomped all over my dream.

He'd have sacrificed it all. What bullshit!

I *am* the goddamn sacrifice!

But the clincher?

God, the stupid fucking crowning glory of it all…

I'm still in love with the jackass.

My heart—which was never meant to be part of this deal—is still in the palm of his hands. And he's crushing it. Every time I think of how easily he walked away from me last night—chose his horrible family over me, abandoned me—another piece of its fragile core breaks away.

I'm still standing there, staring at the empty space where my heart once beat, when Daddy pulls into the drive.

He drifts up the porch, patting me on the shoulder on his way by, and ambles over to sit in his favorite rocking chair—the one my mother used to inhabit every summer night.

"Come. Sit," he demands, his craggy voice showing no hint of emotion.

I don't bother hiding my tears. I simply flop down in the seat beside him, allowing the salty streams of misery to drip down my chin.

"You were right," I tell him, clutching at the ache in my chest.

"And you're admitting it? Better mark this on the calendar," he quips, tipping his chair back.

I laugh through my tears, the sound strangled and pathetic.

"Tell me."

"Brooks, the Kincaides, and all the things you warned me about…you were right. He's rotten. They all are."

"Afraid I'm going to have to disagree with you this time."

"What?" I croak, shooting him an unbelieving glare.

He stares back with cool confidence. It's the look of a man

who understands the world and his place in it. A look of conviction.

"Brooks is different from the rest of 'em. He's a good man. A hell of a lot better than his devil of a father. I've seen it firsthand. Seen and heard how much he respects you. Hell, he actually listens to Hank and all his yammering about them damn horses."

"You weren't there last night. You didn't see how he trampled over the deal we made." I clutch my chest, which feels like it's cracking in two. "He broke his promise to me, Daddy."

"No, you're right, I wasn't there." He tips his chair forward, stopping to lean just a little closer to me and holding my gaze the entire time. "But sometimes promises are impossible to keep, no matter how hard we try. It's one screwup, sweetheart, and it doesn't change facts."

"What facts?"

His chair creaks as he sits back and resumes his rocking. "That man loves you, Addison Jean. And if you ask me, that's the only thing that matters."

He looks up to the endless blue sky, and I join him, leaning back in my chair to take in the warm splendor of the summer sun.

I want to believe. I really do. But if Brooks felt that way about me—if he loved me even half as much as I love him—he'd have said it. Wouldn't he?

He certainly wouldn't have walked all over me. Or broken my heart.

Besides, we come from different worlds. Nothing about the Kincaides' grand lifestyle suits me. All the politics, drama, and pretense do nothing more than wear me down. I don't know how he tolerates his gilded cage.

He and I are clearly not a good match.

"You're thinking too hard," Daddy grunts, his voice thick with sleep.

I sigh. "You know me too well, old man."

We're quiet for a while longer, both lost in our own heads until Daddy's breath turns deep and even, and I wonder if a nap would do me some good as well. Only, I'd probably just stare at the ceiling with my mind going in circles and my system swimming in caffeine.

"When your mother left, I did a lot of thinking." Daddy startles me, his words striking hard against my fragile heart. "I wondered what I'd done wrong and how I could fix it. How I could've done things better. Sometimes, I still wish I could show her how much I loved her. But most of all, I wish she could see how much she missed with you."

"Daddy..." New tears blur my vision. "She's not coming back."

"I know. But that's my point, Addie. She didn't even tell me she was leaving. Whatever the problem was, I never had a hope of fixing it because she walked away without giving me an opportunity to try."

I swallow hard, pushing back the pain and thinking of what Brooks said just before he walked away—before I pushed him away.

I'd sacrifice it all if you'd let me.

"Do you regret letting her hurt you that way?"

"I didn't choose it," he huffs. "It's a risk you take when you fall in love."

"That's what I'm afraid of," I admit.

"I know." He nods, his eyes closing on a sigh. "But there's no rewards without risks."

"So, you're saying I should give Brooks a chance to fix things?"

"You said it, sweetheart. Not me."

19

BROOKS

"Well, what do you know, the Devil's son sleeps." My voice comes out like a low, lazy drawl and Ridge jumps in the doorway to his office, looking up from his phone.

I'd expected to find him already working despite the early hour, but the place was empty. I'm sitting in the chair behind the desk and our offices are near identical, mirror images of the other. But somehow, sitting in *his* chair behind *his* desk in *his* office is satisfying in a way it really shouldn't be.

The interloper that I am is invading his space. The worthy one. The prodigal son. But Ridge doesn't know I'm only his half-brother.

Even with this news, he never truly had any more power than I did—well, at least, I never thought he did. That's all about to change and my gut spasms.

Despite spending the better part of a restless night

mulling this over—and it is the right thing to do—surrender sucks. Defeat tastes nastier than a dip of tobacco. Strange mint taste aside, it's like licking an ashtray filled with cigarette butts.

Squinty-eyed and lip curled, Ridge ambles farther into his office and shuts the door behind him. He studies me in the hazy shafts of the rising sun filtering in through the window.

"Why are you in here?"

There's the welcoming tone I love so much.

His bite makes it easier and harder to do this. The other night, after I blurted to Sage that I might walk away from the ranch, the notion wouldn't leave me.

At first, I wondered if being done with Canyon Spring Ranch was about learning I wasn't the blood son of the woman I knew as Mother, but in reality, it didn't change anything. And in some ways, knowing the truth has further released her hold on me.

Then Cole's question from not too long ago—why I wanted the marriage with Addie—kept nagging at me. Even when I spoke to Addie, tried to apologize, all of it just kept spinning around in my head.

And in the dark hours of the night, what I had to do took shape.

It isn't an easy task, like riding roughstock, but with prac- tice and perseverance I will succeed. It's the only thing to do if I want Addie.

And shit, I want her something fierce.

I fucked up, and while she wants—or more like expects

—me to walk away from her and our marriage, it isn't the answer.

It'll be hard, mending fences, but since when has anything ever been easy with Addison Monroe? And I figure it'll make the reward—my wife—all the sweeter when we're a true partnership in both marriage and business.

There's a lot of ground to cover before we get to that point, many more fights and unfortunately maybe even more nights apart, but now more than ever, I'm up for the challenge because I know what I'm fighting for. What is mine.

And unlike at Canyon Spring Ranch, with Addie and her father, my voice is heard and my ideas count. I'm not less than.

We can build something magnificent if only she gives me another chance. I'm just going to have to make her see it's the only solution.

Ridge clears his throat impatiently, and I push up from his chair, no longer needing any of this in order to be fulfilled. "Crack open the moonshine, because brother dear, you have won."

"What are you talking about?" Annoyance oozes from his every pore along with something else—something I can't quite put my finger on—but it's enough to make me stop.

Something's different about him. His arrogant self-assuredness is missing, or maybe just not as prominent as usual. Did Sage tell him about our conversation? And now he feels sorry for me? Fuck it, I don't care, and I won't talk about that with him.

"I'm backing away from Canyon Spring Ranch, stepping

down, washing my hands of it all." I make a point of dusting my hands together to mimic just that.

"Brooks, it's too early in the morning for your games." He sidesteps me to get to his desk, slumping in the leather chair, elbows now perched on the surface. "What the hell are you talking about?"

His hands clutch at either side of his head as if keeping his head up has become just too hard or unbearable for him.

"You won. Pa and Mama, you all won. I don't want anything to do with the ranch, and I'm not only moving out of the family business, but I'm also moving out of the house."

His head snaps up, and his sharp blue eyes focus in on me, unwavering and skeptical. "Seriously?"

Okay. He doesn't know anything about Sage's news.

I nod, pressing my lips together because anything I have to say will only give him a further glimpse at my loss and ultimately, more satisfaction.

"But why?" He stands, palms pressing into the desk.

For the first time, I take a good look at him, seeing that he isn't looking so good himself. In fact, he looks the way I felt after I left Addie's ranch yesterday, beaten and done for.

"I can't play this game anymore." I wave my hand carelessly around the room, signifying this entire place. "All my life, I wanted nothing more than to please Pa, to one day run the ranch and make him proud, but I was a fool."

I edge closer to the door, unable to stop my babbling, something crawling up my throat with an intense, unstoppable need to get it all out even if it strips my soul bare.

"I've never been happy. Not truly happy." I shake my head

as if trying to rid myself of all those dark memories, the very feeling of just not being good enough.

And strangely, knowing Sage isn't my mother doesn't lessen or intensify those feelings. They are what they are, and even though the truth was hidden for my entire life, I bore the brunt of it day in and day out. And I'm done with all of it.

"I finally found happiness, and it's the funniest thing." I snort and don't fight the small smile pushing on the corners of my mouth. "Never have I been as happy as I am with Addie. Never in my entire life. Certainly not when I was doing Pa's dirty work or trying to please him. And while my marriage may have started out as another one of my foolish ways to make that son of a bitch proud, I no longer care about him or this place. What I care about most in this world is building a life where my woman can be happy and proud of me."

"And Addie does that for you?" His tone is weary and maybe even a little envious.

"Yeah, she does. And I'm not going to fuck that up by letting you and Mama ruin it with your crap like the other night at the gala. We're going forward with Greener Prospects, and if I don't have the financial support of Canyon Spring Ranch, we'll remove the name. But either way, Monroe is at least one part of it and will be no matter what."

We stare at each other, the silence thick and heavy. Ridge is the first to move, dropping his chin to his chest and shaking his head.

"Don't you ever get tired of it all?" His words are muffled with his face tucked in.

I cock my head to one side, taken aback by the fatigue and maybe even a bit of shame in his tone.

"Tired?" It's a cautious response, not readily willing to take the bait if that's what this is. I've been duped too many times by Ridge for a lifetime and what for?

All because he's my brother and I only wanted things to be friendly between us. I only wanted my brother to be... well, my brother. And as much as I'd like to dump all the blame on him, I can't. We both played our parts well—too damn well.

"Yeah, tired." He lifts his head, gaze finding mine. "Pa was a mean old bastard and set us against one another." He rakes a hand harshly through his disheveled head of hair. "But just think about what he'd have done if we'd teamed up and done our own shit. Shown him that the Kincaide brothers couldn't be divided."

Both Pa and Sage would have been beside themselves, and the image causes me to laugh. I can't help it, and it isn't a sharp, sarcastic one. No, this is full and easy, loosening the tightness I hadn't realized was banding around my chest. My brother joins me, sharing a rare moment of amusement, before we get ahold of ourselves.

"That would have been something. Shit, you serious?" There's an incredulous and also challenging edge to my voice. "Would you have done that? Ignored Pa, gone against his orders, and partnered with me?"

"No." It's only a word, and it comes out like nearly noth-ing. "I wish I could say I would have, but you and I both know we weren't strong enough. No, *I* wasn't strong enough to do that, and I fucking wish I was."

My brother holds my gaze for several beats. The two of us say so much in that short silence, both of us understanding what we might never truly say out loud, and that's okay because we don't need the words.

We were both there.

We lived our childhood and young adult years, side by side, even if we were enemies.

We are brothers.

We both did wrong but not all is lost.

We can do better.

"Brooks, I can't speak for Mama, but I don't want you to go." He holds up a hand as I open my mouth. "I understand if you have to but know that you'll always be welcomed here. In fact, I'd like to partner with you in running the ranch."

My jaw slackens, and I can't believe my ears. The idea of running things with Ridge is tempting, and what a glorious "fuck you" to Sage that would be. But he could only be spouting words...even more, just the thought of Addie and her reaction, and I know it isn't the path for me.

As if running on the same track, he continues, "And as for Addie, I'll do whatever you need to help you get her back. I'm sorry for the gala, and if you need me to, I'll tell her to her face about my part in stripping the Monroe name from everything." Shame blankets his tone.

"An apology would be appreciated." My fingers curl around the back of a chair, leaning into it. "She deserves it, but you don't need to explain anything to her. I've got enough of that to do for all of us."

"You might also want to do something about Derek."

I straighten, an uneasy churning swirling in my gut. "What about him?"

"Let's just say, in our attempt to ruin your partnership with Addie, it came to light that he's also been sticking his nose where it doesn't belong. Mama jumped on that and got him to create the mess for you with Geyser Tech and the canceled water supplies."

"Go on." My hands tighten into fists, already guessing where this is going but needing to hear all the details.

"He was behind it...well, with Mama's prodding. Frannie was talking at the gala—she feels something awful about the mix-up—and Derek's assistant, Jolene, piped up." He gives me a knowing glance, and I furrow my brow, the woman not easily coming to mind. "You know, the one he fooled around with a while back and then dumped like a hot potato for Addie."

I nod, vaguely recalling the drama that had the entire town fired up. "If I remember correctly, she had a mouth on her and was none too happy. Jolene made sure everyone knew about it."

"Yeah, she sure did. Anyway, at the gala, Jolene bragged to Frannie that she was the one to call Geyser Tech, acting like Addie. She told them to forget about the order. Something about Derek realizing the error of his ways and he wanted to teach Addie a lesson. When I mentioned it to Mama, she confirmed she'd been behind it. She left it up to him as to how or when he'd cause a problem."

"That son of a bitch." Like an erupting volcano, fury flows through me like lava, and the urge to do something about Derek's meddling pulses through my veins.

Sage is the true culprit, but I'm not touching her, no more than I already have. The sooner I'm away from the family business, the less chance of her causing problems. But Derek needs to understand he can't continue messing with me and Addie, no matter who encouraged him.

"I know that look." Ridge dips his chin and arches a brow. "I've seen it far too many times, mostly aimed at me. Give that asshole hell."

"I intend to. Thanks for telling me. I appreciate it." I turn, heading for the door with Derek as my top priority.

But before leaving, I glance back at my brother, an affinity taking hold of my insides. "Ridge, good luck with Pa's will and his requirements. Who knows, you might get lucky like me and find the woman of your dreams."

"Thanks, Brooks, but I'm not going to hold my breath on that. I think having it all might be a bit too much to ask—even for me." He sinks into the chair and powers on his computer, done with the conversation.

I meant what I said; I hope Ridge does head Canyon Spring with all success. My belief in him, his ability to turn things around and pave a more harmonious way to prosperity, has always been there. Maybe a little stunted in growth, and at times, it nearly died, but now more than ever, I believe if anyone can do it, he can.

"**Y**ou mother—"

I grab Derek by his shirt collar, yanking him

from a booth in The Crispy Biscuit and cutting his words short.

Conversation stops, and several of the patrons release surprised gasps with one woman, I think Pastor Richardson's wife, saying, "My dear Lord."

"What the hell?" Derek snarls and curls his hand around my forearm, trying to loosen my hold.

Rage quickens my blood, and I don't budge. We have an audience, and it should give me pause, but I couldn't care less. I made a huge mistake in blaming Addie for the canceled order when this piece of shit was at fault.

And while not fully to blame, he's going to get my wrath.

It took longer than expected to find the weasel, and while I'd like to say I hesitated when I learned of his whereabouts, I never gave it a moment's thought.

This may not be smart, confronting Derek during the breakfast rush in the town's only diner, but he needs to understand this bullshit and his meddling stop now.

At first, I'd gone to his office where Jolene, his assistant and fuck buddy, gave up his location all too easily. She was sweet as pie with not a hint of the smugness Ridge spoke of, tripping over herself and all too accommodating of my need to kick her boss's butt.

"Boys, take it outside." Skeeter Jones, six feet four and two hundred eighty pounds of solid muscle, ambles from the kitchen.

He's a decorated veteran with the sharpest shot and the meanest griddling skills in town. And even as he pushes sixty, the guy could knock us both out flat without even batting an eyelash.

"All right, Skeet, we're going." My grip tightens on Derek's shirt as I haul him from the diner.

Many lookie-loos gawk, and some even have the audacity to get up from their tables and follow us out onto the sidewalk. I suppose I am giving them a show.

"Let go of me." Derek tries to wriggle free, but I've got him good.

"I'm not wasting any more time or breath on you than necessary." I release my hold, and he nearly falls onto his ass, not expecting the move.

"Fuck off, Brooks."

My irritation flares, and I drag in a deep breath, trying not to let my anger cloud my judgement any further. I screwed up with Addie, and I'll have to make that right, but we don't need the likes of this idiot making things any more difficult between us than they already are.

"The stunt you pulled with Geyser Tech—you're going to get a bill for the entire order." I lean in real close, our foreheads practically touching as my finger pokes at his chest, a jab for every word. "And you will pay it."

"Like hell I will." He tries to sidestep me, but I'm on him like glue.

"I thought we had an understanding, but it seems you're not only stupid but also hard of hearing." My hand whacks him lightly upside his head, unable to resist the move.

He growls, baring his teeth and nostrils flaring, but he doesn't come for me. Rather, he glances furtively to the left and right of him at the gathering crowd. "You need to know that I wasn't the only one."

"Shut up," I bellow, not wanting him to mention Sage.

While I'd like nothing more than to show that woman for the conniving witch she is, I won't hurt my family. We're already giving the townsfolk something to talk about, but I won't tear down the Kincaide name, because no matter what Sage believes, I'm not less than. I am a Kincaide.

"You stay away from my wife and out of our business. You so much as see us walking on the same sidewalk as you, then you cross the street. Got it?"

"It's a free country, Brooks. The Kincaides don't own this fucking town." His anger, but also something else, maybe fear, crackles in the air around him.

"Listen, jackass. I could have played this a number of ways." Thoughts of beating him to a pulp, still vivid and tempting, run through my mind. "But I thought I'd appeal to you, one businessman to another."

I straighten, now my turn to take in the crowd as I make eye contact with a few people. What I'm about to say isn't arrogance; it's fact, and I want these people gathered around to understand that.

"I've got more pull in this town than you'll ever hope to have." With a few nods of agreement from those around us, I sharpen my gaze on Derek. "All it'll take is one word from me to shut you down. Not another living soul in the state of Montana will do business with you. You understand?"

He swallows hard, nodding imperceptibly and paling. I might be imagining it, but he also shrinks.

"So long as I've made myself clear." My hands slap against the front of his jacket a little too hard, and it sends him stumbling backward. "We're done here."

20

ADDISON

"*H*ey, Addie!" Hank calls as I stroll aimlessly toward the corral, where he's already got Missy out, trotting circles.

I couldn't stand to sit around the house and mope a minute longer. Three days of wallowing in misery of my own making is long enough—I was starting to irritate myself. Poor Daddy must be out of his mind by now.

"If you're here for Brooks, you just missed him."

I stumble into the fence, leaning on it for support. "Brooks was here?"

Dammit. One mention of his name and I'm a puddle of goo.

It's only been three days since I sent him packing, but I haven't stopped thinking about him—his generosity, cocky attitude, gloriously big hands, and every other detail are on my mind constantly.

It doesn't help that everything reminds me of him. He's

touched every part of this ranch in one way or another, and it all feels so lacking, so empty without him here.

"Yeah." Hank doesn't bother looking my way. He's too busy watching his pride and joy prance in front of him. "He let me know the water recycling program was delayed. Guess there was a mix-up with the Geyser Tech supply order?"

"Wait." My eyes track Missy around the ring, my head spinning to fit pieces together. "He's setting up a water program...here?"

Hank turns to me with a sheepish look, removing his hat and scratching his head. "Dang it. I wasn't supposed to tell you that part, was I?"

A throbbing pulse bangs to life at the base of my skull. "And you're helping him? When did you set this up?"

"About a little over two weeks ago? It was meant to be a surprise. Guess I blew it."

Missy stomps a hoof, adding a shrill whinny to the conversation and drawing Hank's attention. She really is a little devil, and it's fun to see her give my cousin a hard time, but even her cute antics can't ease the pressure on my mind.

After my talk with Daddy, I've thought about giving Brooks a chance to make things right. I've wondered if I was too hard on him, too quick to judge, and whether he could somehow make it up to me.

Could I forgive him for so brutally breaking my trust? For putting Canyon Spring Ranch and his family first?

But now, I see...second chances are for fools. If Mama strolled up here tomorrow, Daddy would forgive her. He'd put aside the wreckage of his heart and welcome her back with open arms. And for what? More hurt? More heartbreak?

Is that what I want for my life?

Hank has unwittingly revealed a new layer to Brooks's deception. Proof that he went behind my back at least two weeks ago. But how far back does the treachery go? Did he plan to undermine me from the start?

And does his plan to take over Greener Prospects run even deeper? Is he planning to take over my ranch?

The edge of the wood fence splinters under my grip, and I push myself to stand straight—on my own two feet.

"It's good," I tell Hank. "I'm not a big fan of surprises." Especially not when they're meant to screw me over.

If Brooks Kincaide thinks he's going to come in here, take over Greener Prospects, and run me out of my own business, he's out of his damn mind.

"He didn't happen to mention where he was going, did he, Hank?"

"No, but he headed back toward Canyon Spring."

"Thanks." I stalk away from my blissfully unaware cousin and his devil horse, muttering curses at him under my breath.

Fuck. I'm shooting mad, but I can't hold this against Hank. If anything, he's a victim too, tricked into believing he was helping bring my plans to life.

Who would have guessed I was being duped by my own husband?

Me. I should have known. If I'd kept my panties on and guard up, I'd never have fallen into this mess. I'd never have started to feel...anything.

At the stables, I can see Tink's muzzle peeking over her

stall door, and my temper fades. "Hey, girl," I coo, not wanting her to feel the residuals of my frustration.

She noses me, searching my pockets for a treat, and instantly I'm smiling.

"Let's go for a ride."

There are acres of land between us, but it doesn't take long for the top of the Canyon Spring estate to come into view. The house is so disgustingly ostentatious, it's a wonder I can't see it from my front porch.

Brooks and I really do come from two different worlds. And I really can't say I like his much. Sure, it's pretty to look at, but I know underneath the shiny veneer is a hollow den of arrogance, fraud, and greed.

I'll be much better off leaving this all behind.

Tink picks up the pace, almost like she can read my mind and knows how anxious I am to get there. Like my mission to tell Brooks off, to set him straight about my business and my ranch, is just as important to her as it is to me.

"Good girl." I softly tug her reins, directing her to the side of the Kincaide family home, where an elaborate hitching post is set.

I'm taking the front steps two at a time when it dawns on me, I didn't even look in a mirror. My hair is in a wild, windswept tail. My jeans are dirty, and my shirt's a sweaty, tight-fitting T. My face...dear Lord, my face is probably still stained with tears from the past three days.

Fuck it.

I push through the door without knocking. This is Brooks's home. I'm his wife. I should be welcome here, even if I was never made to feel it.

My boots clomp over the hardwood, leaving a trail of dust in my wake. No point in hiding my presence or worrying over a little dirt. There are far more pressing issues at hand. The door to Brooks's office is closed, but that doesn't stop me from barging straight ahead. The well-oiled hinges don't protest my force, and the heavy oak swings open, colliding with a thud against the wall.

Startled—and looking a bit like I've caught her doing something she shouldn't be—Scarlett stares at me from behind the desk, her eyes wide and mouth hanging open.

"Shit, Addie!" Her manicured fingers flutter over her collarbone. "You nearly gave me a heart attack."

Her eyes close on a heavy sigh, her lips mashing together in a tight line, and her chin begins to quiver.

What the hell? Is she going to cry? Because I scared her?

"It's just a stupid saying." She sniffles. "Like a reflex, really...and heck, I didn't even like the man. But...but I still can't help feeling like I just committed some sort of sacrilege. Like he's somehow going to punish me from his grave." She looks to me with tears in her eyes. "How ridiculous is that?"

Shit. She's talking about Devlin. Her father's heart attack and sudden death must have been a shock to them all. Obviously, Scarlett's still processing it.

"It's not ridiculous, and I'm sorry. I wasn't expecting to find you in here. I was looking for Brooks."

She dabs at the corners of her eyes. "You must think I'm silly for reacting this way."

"About as silly as me banging down your door."

"He really fucked things up, didn't he?" she says through

a laugh. "I love my big brother, but God, he can be such a blind idiot."

The tension seeps from my body, and I take a seat in front of her, leaning my elbows on the desk. "He really did. Fuck things up, that is."

"Addie, I realize I'm younger than you and we don't know each other well, but I feel like I should give you some advice."

"Advice?"

"Brooks is loyal to a fault. In the past, that meant doing whatever my father told him for the betterment of this ranch and our family. Or so he was told. He tried so hard to make that man proud of him. To live up to an impossible standard. Pa might be gone, but Brooks has still been trying to prove himself."

She reaches across the desk, covering my hand with hers and spearing me with the sincerity of her gaze. "Only, things changed once you came into the picture, Addie."

"They did?" I lean in, holding my breath.

"He's still loyal—that'll never change—but his allegiance has shifted. Now, he's trying to prove himself to you."

I pull away, exhaling loudly as I slump back in my chair. "If that were true, he wouldn't have taken all the credit for Greener Prospects. He wouldn't have gone behind my back and made me look a fool in front of the whole town."

"No, he wouldn't." Her words are absolute, her tone exact.

My chest fills with a surge of hope, but I press it down, not ready to face more disappointment. "What are you saying? That he didn't do anything wrong?"

"No, he definitely messed up. Just not the way you're

thinking. His mistake was putting faith in the values of a dead man and trusting Mama to do the right thing. He's been striving for control of something he doesn't really want, when the thing he does is staring him in the face." Her eyes narrow on me. "Maybe you should meet him halfway."

Tears fill my eyes, and I shake my head—unable or perhaps just unwilling to believe what she's saying.

"But the event," I croak. "The banners…"

"Oh, that was Mama and Ridge." She waves a hand through the air, like it was obvious and not a big deal at all.

"Pardon?" My stomach tumbles.

"They switched it all at the last minute. Brooks had no idea."

My mind flashes back to the moment at the gala when I pointed it out to him and the look of shock on his face. I'd thought he was putting on an act, playing his mother's wicked game, and lying to keep me on his arm long enough to secure his seat at Canyon Spring Ranch.

But God, I was wrong. So very, very wrong.

And if I was wrong about that…what else?

Certainly not Sage—I was right to think the woman is as cold as they come. Still, to sabotage her own son takes a special kind of ruthlessness. A savagery only the most broken seem to possess.

"What about the water recycling plan at my ranch?" I persist, poking holes in Scarlett's story. Risk may come with reward, but it also comes with consequence, and I'm still not sure if I can take the chance.

"I don't know anything about that." She shrugs. "But

maybe you should talk to him about it. Maybe you'll find out the two of you aren't as far apart on this thing as you think."

She leans back in her chair, running a hand over her sleek, dark hair, reminding me of what a disaster I must look.

"I should go," I mumble, getting to my feet, but pause. "I'm sorry, Scarlett. I think I might have misjudged you."

"It's okay." She waves me off. "Everyone does."

"Well, I'm sorry for that, too," I say, sincerely.

Her lips tilt up and her expression softens into what may be the first true smile I've ever seen from her. "Thanks."

The ride back home takes twice as long, much to Tink's dismay. But it's hard to concentrate with my mind in knots, and distracted riding is a good way to get myself, my horse, or both of us hurt.

So much has happened in such a short time, and there's still much more to come.

By the time I reach our stables, my decision is made. My plan clear.

Hank's right where I left him, and I waste no time, riding straight up beside him. "I need your help."

He looks up to me with a grin, ten times the size of normal. "I've been waiting to hear you admit it."

"I know," I grit, my stubborn streak still wanting to rear its defensive and misguided head. "You can rub it in later. Right now, I need you and your big mouth to help me get in touch with all the ranchers who've signed contracts with Greener Prospects."

"Okay..." he drawls. "What exactly for?"

"I've got a new proposition for them."

21

BROOKS

"Uh-huh, I figured you'd come around sooner or later with your hat in hand." George sways back and forth in the rocking chair, smirking at the Stetson I just pulled off my head. "Only, I'm surprised it took you this long."

I shake my head, holding back my frown at his rebuke, and look to the ground like I've been scolded. The toe of my boot kicks a small pebble across the dusty, wooden porch. I'm stalling, prolonging the inevitable.

"Well, you just going to stand there or get to it?" He hooks his weathered chin in the direction of the front door. "She's inside."

The hand raking through my sweat-disheveled hair stops, and a chill prickles along my spine. Addie's inside, only some feet from where I stand, and the strangest sensation squeezes my chest.

What I'd give to lay eyes on her...

Nope, not going to give in to the urge, or not just yet, anyway. This visit to Monroe ranch is about Addie but also George, and I need to deal with him first.

If I'm to stand another chance with Addie, I've got to do this right. Sorry wasn't enough for her. Shit. I'm not even sure how many chances she'll give me. If I even get one…but I'm not giving up.

"Um." I clear my throat and look him square in the eye. "I'll go in shortly. I wanted to have a word with you first. I apologized to Addie the other day—"

"You did?" He sits up a little straighter, shaking off his lazy, *haven't got a care in the world* disguise.

Mentally, the old man is quicker than a whip and doesn't miss much. While he won't interfere in my marriage or the business partnership Addie and I started, his daughter's happiness is most important.

"Yeah, it didn't go so well. She figured it wasn't enough and…" My thumb glides along the brim of my hat.

"Not surprised." He shakes his head and lets out a low grunt of disapproval.

"Anyway, I owe you an apology, too."

His blue gaze sharpens. "What for? You did nothing to me."

"Yeah, I did. Addison and I went into this marriage for many reasons, and as time went on, things changed for me. The way I feel about your daughter grew and deepened." I straighten my shoulders and inject as much sincerity into my voice as is possible. "I love her, and I want our marriage to work."

He nods but keeps his mouth shut, watching me mosey over to one side of the porch, closer to him.

I perch my ass on the railing. "And I've grown to respect you, look up to you, and even look forward to our talks."

He fidgets in his chair, never breaking eye contact as a flush creeps into his cheeks. "No need to get mushy on me."

"I promise not to cry." I chuckle to make light of the situation and blink away the burning in my eyes.

Damn, this man better not make a liar out of me and bring me to tears.

"What I'm trying to say is, I went into this marriage with an agenda. We both did, and even when I started to feel and believe differently than what had been drilled into me from a young age—about you and the Monroes—I was a fool. I tried to push all that aside and never wavered from that agenda."

"Agenda?" He leans forward, trembling a bit, and I can't shake the feeling he knows exactly what I'm talking about but has every intention of drawing it out of me.

He wants me to say the words, and I can't blame him. He deserves this revelation, for lack of a better word. He sure as shit would never have gotten it from my father when he was alive. Not to say Devlin Kincaide was enlightened enough to agree with my thinking.

"My loyalty has always been to Canyon Spring and my family, and my relationship with Addie had initially been about them. About proving I was the best man to run the ranch."

I awkwardly shift from one boot to the other, suddenly hotter than a branding iron. Why is talking about feelings so hard?

"Anyway, I can't say I'll turn my back on them." I swallow hard and my conversation with Ridge comes back to me, both the release and melancholy still very much tugging at my insides.

"Of course. They're your family." George nods and offers a relaxed smile, as if sensing my unease at admitting this... this failure.

I don't want to call it that—not because of pride, but more because I tried. I went above and beyond but never stood a chance at securing my spot as head of the family. Never.

And this line of thinking is senseless and not why I came here. I scratch at the back of my neck and once again lock eyes with my father-in-law.

"Sure, they're family, but I've got a better, truer family right here. With you and Addison. And I'm sorry it took me so long to realize it."

I stick my hand out for him to shake, and at first, he just stares at it like my appendage is some foreign object. Then his resolute gaze shifts to my face, and he goes back and forth between the two for what feels like eternity.

Maybe I read him wrong, and when I thought he was taking me under his wing, treating me like a son, he was only doing what was right for his daughter.

Finally, with much effort, he pushes to his feet and shuf-fles to me, grabbing my hand in a firm grip. His other gnarly hand wallops my back in some kind of gruff acceptance—a man's hug, if I can call it that.

"Well, in that case, I owe you an apology, too." He's grin-ning, but his tone is serious, and I wrinkle my brow, cocking my head to one side. "I was wrong. Not all of Devlin Kincaide's offspring are evil incarnate. That son of a bitch did something right with you because you're one fine man, and I'm proud to have you as a son-in-law."

My chest swells with a warmth and pride I had only ever hoped to receive from my old man. But this is better. This is George.

"Thank you, sir."

His hand drops from mine, and he steps back as his smile grows wider. "You sure you weren't adopted or delivered by the stork?"

That gets another chuckle from both of us, only George has no idea how close he is to the truth.

He slides his arms behind his back in what's become one of his signature moves. It's not a casual gesture; it's more like he's hiding something, and it gives me pause when he sobers.

"Since we're busy being honest...Brooks, I'm getting old, and I think you've noticed my body's failing me. Well, I've got Parkinson's. Not many know, and I'd like to keep it like that for as long as I can, but since you're family, I thought you should know."

I nod, pressing my lips into a firm line while I search for the right words that won't come off like pity. Things now make sense—Addie's concern for her father and those moments when he appeared frail or ailing.

But before I can utter a sound, George says roughly, clearly wanting to move past his confession, "What are you going to do about Addie?"

"Besides a lot of groveling?" I take the opportunity to lighten the mood, and one side of my mouth tips up into a wry grin. "I wanted to ask you about any destinations she has dreamed about visiting. Any ideas where she'd love to go? I want to take her on a honeymoon."

"Hold your horses." He props his hands on his leather-belted waist. "What makes you think she needs a honeymoon when she didn't even have a proper wedding?"

Dumbfounded, the words tumble around in my mind. "You're right. Why didn't I think about that?"

"Because I'm the smart one." He slaps my shoulder again and winks. "You love my daughter, it's plain to see. So, make it official for the entire town to see. It'll go a long way with her, and as an added bonus, it might just get rid of the dirty dog, Derek, too."

My jaw tightens at the mention of her ex even as the idea takes shape in my mind. "It's a great idea."

"I know. I came up with it." He lumbers back to the rocking chair. "And just so you know, Hank told me what you did with that water program or whatever it is you're doing for the ranch."

"He can't keep his mouth shut, can he?" I glance out to the barn where Hank most probably is at this very moment.

"Nope. The poor man never met a secret he could keep. Don't be mad at him." George rests his head on the back of the seat, rocking, and shuts his eyes.

"I'm not upset with Hank." I inch toward the door with Addie as my top priority. "Well, if you'll excuse me."

He dips his chin, eyes shutting once more, and he murmurs something unintelligible as I walk through the door to the house. Sounds from the kitchen give me an idea as to where I might find Addie, and sure enough, she's at the sink, washing what looks to be a large glass bowl.

She places the item in the drainboard and turns for a towel, pausing in midstride at the sight of me. Her cheeks immediately heat, turning the prettiest shade of pink, and her eyes widen.

"What are you doing here?" she snaps, pursing her lips and pulling the towel from the rack on the wall.

"Hello, my lovely wife." My lopsided, flirty grin does nothing to soften her tough exterior. "Look, I didn't like how we ended things the other day, and while I left, I never gave up."

She slaps the towel onto the counter and marches closer to me, fire in her steps. Her mouth opens, jaw set, but then she clamps it shut as if thinking better of it. I take her silence as my opportunity to forge ahead.

"I'm sorry." I'm quick to raise up my hand when she opens her mouth again. "And I know that for you, that isn't enough. I heard you and I get it, but I wanted to say it again. I'm sorry for everything. For how we got started, going into this as a business arrangement instead of a relationship, and how I thought you interfered with an order, and—"

"Brooks, what are you saying?" Her voice is low, expression now slack, almost defeated, and it's clear to see she's taking my words the wrong way.

"I'm done with Canyon Spring Ranch." It comes out a blurted, breathless exclamation, like some teenager with barely the balls to ask the girl he likes to dance.

There's so much more to tell her, including Sage's news, and I will, but not now. My decision to leave the ranch behind has nothing to do with that revelation, and I don't want her thinking it does.

I don't want my wife believing the only reason I'm one hundred percent behind the Monroes, their ranch, and Greener Prospects is because I'm not Sage's biological son.

That couldn't be further from the truth. All I want is Addie and a life with her.

"What?" Addie shakes her head, taking another step toward me, and as her heady scent hits me everywhere, it takes everything in me not to grab her and hold her close. "What does that mean? Done?"

"I told Ridge he can have it, everything. I'll never get to run the ranch, and truth be told, I don't want to run it." I place my hat on the counter and stare down at her earnestly. "They'll always be my family. I can't change that, but they're no longer the most important thing in my life. You are."

My hand reaches for her, but she stiffens. Okay, too soon.

"You are my wife, and I want us to have a partnership in every sense of the word. I want to work on Greener Prospects with you—equal partners—and help with this ranch...that is, if you'll have me."

Addie folds her arms over her chest even as her expression softens. She's pulling up the barricades, getting ready to bolt, even if part of her doesn't want to. I feel the chill of her impending absence in my bones.

Oh, no, she doesn't.

I brace one hand on the counter and get down on one knee, taking her warm, slender hand in mine. Confusion, shock, and maybe even a flash of excitement cloud her pretty green eyes.

"Darlin', will you marry me?"

"Brooks?" Even with the worry and maybe a touch of fear in her expression, her fingers curl around mine. "What are you doing?"

"Well, what does it look like I'm doing? I'm asking you to marry me."

"But...but..." Her head shakes, and silky blonde locks sway from side to side. "We're already married."

"Sure, we are in the eyes of the law." I tighten my hold as her fingers slide back a bit, as if retreating from my grasp. "But our marriage isn't about some business arrangement. It may have started out that way, but if we're both being honest, us, this right here is about a whole lot more than business."

I dip my head, catching her gaze as she tries to look away. "I love you. Forget about Canyon Spring and Greener Prospects. I want us to do this right, and I want you to have it all. The big wedding, the gown, flowers...you name it. And I want everyone to see just how ridiculously happy you make me."

She nibbles on her lips, brow wrinkling as she studies me like I'm some puzzle to be solved. She remains silent, and it's killing me.

"Darlin', I'm not great at reading minds. What do you say? Is it a yes?"

22

ADDISON

I think I might be in shock. Brooks is down on one knee, his blue eyes sparkling with sincerity, and I'm pretty sure the words that just came out of his mouth—the ones after he asked me to marry him—were "I love you." But my heart is beating so loudly, I don't trust I heard him right.

"I need to tell you something," I blurt, sweat trickling down the back of my neck.

His hopeful expression falls, and his grip on my hand loosens just a fraction.

"Actually, I need to show you something." I tug on his hand, urging him to his feet.

We don't have far to go—the stuffed manila envelope is only steps away, on the kitchen table.

"What's this?"

I keep my head down, unable to look him in the eyes. "I had some legal papers drawn up."

"Legal papers?" He plucks at the corner of the envelope but doesn't open it, and I realize I can't hold him in suspense any longer.

"It's new contracts, and there are more coming. I could only get a few finalized right away—lawyers take forever with this stuff, even when you throw around the Kincaide family name."

"Addie, what the hell are you talkin' about?"

"Daddy told me I should give you a chance to fix things—that if I loved you, it was worth letting you back in. Worth taking a risk. But he was wrong."

His brow furrows with question and maybe a trace of hurt, but I barrel on. "What I need to do is meet you halfway. I've made just as many mistakes, and you're taking just as big a risk. It's not fair to ask you to do all the fixing."

"Darlin'..." His voice trails off and he inches closer, cupping my cheek in his hand—that glorious rough and rugged hand.

"All the Greener Prospects contracts have been amended. The ranchers have all agreed to put a wastewater recycling program in place, ahead of the solar fences. Well, not Jimmy Smith, but he's still mad at me for wanting to punch him, so that's not a surprise."

My heart's racing, trying to keep up with my words. "We even managed to get two new contracts, just from word of mouth. Water recycling is a much bigger deal than I initially thought. You were right. And I'm sorry."

"What?" he chokes out through an unbelieving laugh, his fingers threading into my hair. "What did you just say?"

"About the wastewater?" I ask, breathless.

The blue eyes I adore so much darken to something fierce, almost feral, turning me on in an instant.

"No, darlin'," he growls.

My thighs rub together, and I bite the side of my lip, holding back a moan. "You were right?"

He shakes his head, a sexy smirk playing on his lips. "No, the last part."

Heat coils in my belly, and I stand on my toes to wrap my arms around his neck, drawing our bodies flush. Inch by glorious inch, we align—my breasts tingling, core clenching, and his arousal growing thick between us.

He always brings out the wild thing in me. Feeling bold, I stroke my tongue up the column of his neck, over his pounding pulse, and nip at the base of his jaw, before whispering in his ear, "I'm sorry."

His lips meet mine, and next thing I know, the contracts are scattered on the floor, and I'm pinned to the table with the bulge in Brooks's pants thrusting against my soaked panties.

He hovers over me, holding me down yet lifting me higher. "So, now is that a yes?"

❧

The fingers of my free hand hover over my collarbone, and I stare into Brooks's fixed blue gaze, which seems endless as a clear Montana sky. Breath catches in my lungs, my pulse races, and my head spins with the giddy sensation.

So, this is what it's like to swoon.

His hold on my hand is tender yet fierce and radiates a truth I think I've always known. I can trust him. This man is solid, steady, reliable, and refused to walk away, even when I pushed him. He loves me.

And I'm in love with him.

His thumb presses a reassuring stroke along my skin, and I take a deep breath, relishing our connection. This feeling... *God*, I never want it to end.

Never want to let him go.

He slips the ring on my finger for a second time, and my heart rejoices in the comforting knowledge that I never have to.

He and I are bound together forever.

"I now pronounce you husband and wife," Pastor Richardson announces with zeal, and the group of our family and friends, clustered together in the field behind our home, erupts into enthusiastic applause.

When Brooks got down on one knee in my kitchen, only three weeks ago, I was struck by an odd sense of déjà vu. Not because he was asking me to marry him for a second time, but because the scene played out exactly how my pre-teen fantasies had always imagined—back when romantic daydreams and frilly scrapbooks were part of my every day. Back before my mother left and I closed my heart to the possibility of love.

What he asked me for that day wasn't based on a selfish bargain or even a mutually agreeable business deal. It was based on love. Pure, blinding devotion. He wanted me to share my life with him—to share a life together—and in that moment I couldn't think of anything I wanted more.

Not even Greener Prospects.

I still can't think of anything better.

"Kiss her!" Cole yells from over Brooks's shoulder, and someone lets out a loud wolf whistle.

Laughter bubbles through me, and Brooks's deep chuckle mingles with it, sounding a bit like a symphony, and making me swoon harder as I stare up at the most handsome, loving, and sincere man I've ever met. *My husband.*

With a huge smile lighting him from the inside out, he grasps my face in those hardworking hands I won't ever get enough of, and leans in.

"Gladly," he murmurs, just before his mouth crashes to mine in an urgent sweep of lips, tongues, and teeth.

I let out a completely inappropriate moan, given the company we're in, and someone in the crowd hollers for us to get a room.

Already got one, I think. Only this time around, instead of a fancy, big-city hotel suite, we've got Hannah's remote mountainside cabin to look forward to.

Three days of solitude in wedded bliss with my husband. What could be better than that?

We reluctantly break apart, and Pastor Richardson introduces us to our guests for the first time as a married couple.

Hand-in-hand, we wade into the sea of familiar faces, from Hank who's sitting with my granny Gertrude, to Sheriff Gilbert, Ruby, and Hopper. Brooks's entire family is here as well, including Ridge and his brand-new fiancée, Chastity— who if you ask me, looks a little too much like a younger, snootier version of Sage for comfort. *Seriously, it's creepy.*

Heck, even Jimmy Smith put aside our little spat to be here.

Okay, so maybe a few more guests RSVP'd than I'd expected. Once again, it seems everyone's shown up for us. In fact, people were calling me up, asking when they'd get their invitation, and what I'd assumed would be an intimate family affair has turned into the event of the season.

The crowd gathers around us, congratulating us like we're a celebrity couple. Although I guess in a sense we are. At least to the town of Prospect.

And not just because our story got around—I mean, of course it did, there really aren't many secrets in this place— but because of the work we're doing with our green initiative. The whole town is buzzing about how Greener Prospects is saving ranches, healing the environment, and going to make the townsfolk famous.

Yes, famous.

Somehow, the rumor mill spread so far past our quaint borders, it hit the ears of some Hollywood execs. Now we've got producers interested in turning Prospect's history into a TV miniseries.

Parker swears he had nothing to do with it, but something tells me there's a loophole to his story.

Still, I can't find it in me to be upset about the gossip. For once, I don't mind being the talk of the town.

"Never thought I'd see this day." Daddy pumps Brooks's arm in a hearty handshake, with a sheen of tears in his eyes.

"I know," Brooks agrees. "Never imagined you'd accept a Kincaide as part of your family."

"Me, neither." I burrow into Brooks's chest, gazing up at him with a full heart.

"Well, that, I guess…" Daddy drawls. "But I meant seeing Addie tied down. Never thought she'd find a man who could keep up with her."

Brooks's chest vibrates with his raucous laughter, and I give Daddy the stink-eye for a moment before he drags me in for a hug.

"I'm proud of you, sweetheart." He squeezes me as tight as his old frail arms allow. "And I'm happy for you."

"Thank you, Daddy," I sniffle, wiping tears from my eyes. "None of this would be possible without you."

"No crying before pictures!" Hannah rushes toward us, running a hand over her auburn locks. "I'm already a mess."

Laughing, I pull her in for a tight hug. "You're gorgeous, as always, but I'm sure Scarlett can fix us up. She's a genius with this stuff."

"Thank you," Scarlett calls from over my shoulder. "But I'm not a miracle worker, so let's keep the tears to a minimum."

We all laugh some more and share another round of hugs —even Scarlett gets in on the action. I'd been a little hesitant about asking her to stand as a bridesmaid at our wedding, but her bright look of excitement when I did set my nerves at ease. Her smiles that day were all natural and full, just like the one she's wearing now.

"Excuse me, everyone," Sage urges. "The photographer is waiting."

She holds her head high, her haughty look of arrogance still perfectly in place, but she's at least been subdued and hasn't tried to interfere. Not that she has a reason to anymore.

She got what she wanted. Brooks has stepped aside and given her and Ridge the room to run Canyon Spring Ranch the way she always wanted.

Plus, we know her secret.

Brooks isn't her son, her husband was unfaithful, and her entire life has been built around covering up the lie. Although, I wasn't all that shocked when Brooks told me—it actually makes a hell of a lot of sense.

In some ways, I feel sorry for my mother-in-law. She doesn't seem very happy. Thankfully, her sourness will now stay in its own lane and out of mine.

She certainly won't disrupt the bright mood of this day.

We pose for what feels like a million and one photos, but none are forced. Even Daddy, who needs to sit partway through because of his condition, has a great time hamming it up for the camera.

After pictures, the group of us head for the reception, but Brooks grabs hold of my hand, slowing my stride so that we fall behind Daddy, Sage, and the wedding party.

"On the count of three, get ready to run," he whispers in my ear. "One..."

I laugh. "What on earth—"

"Two..."

"Brooks, I—"

"Three!" he hisses, and takes off running, dragging me along with him.

We break away from the rest of the group, who continue heading toward the barn, where music and laughter spill into the early evening, and run to the open stable, which is quiet and dark.

Once inside, with the smell of fresh hay and the soft sounds of the content horses, Brooks turns to me, cupping my face in his hands, and stares into the depths of my soul.

"There you are," he murmurs.

"I've been here all day," I say through a light laugh.

"I know, but I needed a moment alone with you to really take it all in. You're gorgeous, my little darlin' wife. Stunning."

"Why, thank you." I run my hands up his chest, my breath picking up pace with each inch that disappears from between us. "You're not too terrible to look at, either."

He grunts, threading his fingers into my hair and pulling me even closer. "I'm going to ruin all that pretty makeup now, darlin'."

Before I can even think to protest, his mouth moves over mine in a slow burning kiss that is all-consuming. With this kiss, he worships me. Claims me.

And I give myself over to it. To him.

"Let's skip the party," he growls in my ear, his hands roaming down my body. "I want you out of this dress."

"Brooks!" I yelp when he grabs my ass and starts pulling up my skirt.

Tink blows a loud breath from her stall, letting us know she's not amused, and I laugh. "It's our party. We have to at least put in an appearance. Besides, don't you want to hear Cole give his speech? I bet it's going to be a hilarious disaster."

With a frustrated groan, Brooks concedes, "Fine. We'll go. But first, I'm gonna make you come."

Somehow, his magic hands find their way under the layers of tulle, into my lace panties, and within minutes, he has me clinging to his broad shoulders as I chant his name, orgasming around his fingers.

"I love you, Addison Monroe-Kincaide," he whispers to me in the dark, holding me close as I come down from my high. "And if you promise to love me forever, I'm never letting you go."

"It's a deal." I look up to his handsome face, smiling at the mix of love and lust I see written in the crease of his brow.

After doing our best to clean up at the stable sink under the dim lighting, we sneak back toward the barn, the now starlit sky shining brightly overhead.

"Is that Ridge?" He's following behind a prim, willowy blonde, with his head bowed, hands on his hips and looking like he's being led to slaughter. "And is that Chastity dragging him to the party?"

Brooks snickers, "Doesn't look too happy about it, does he?"

"He looks completely miserable." Nothing like the confident, almost cocky man I've known him to be. "Do you think he's really going to marry her?"

"I have no idea." Brooks wraps his arm around my waist, steering me toward the party. "Ridge is a big boy, and he's choosing his bed. If this is the one he wants to lie in, that's his business."

"Okay. You're right."

But curiosity and maybe a bit of concern tug at me, and I

can't help but wonder if this is truly what he wants for his future. A loveless marriage is one thing, but this seems like he'd be subjecting himself to torture.

Then again, he's probably used to it with Sage.

The music and voices of our guests grow louder, and I push thoughts of Ridge and his troubles away, fussing with my dress one last time before Brooks pulls me into the light of the open doorway.

"Just remember," he murmurs in my ear. "This was your idea."

"Sure," I say through a laugh. "But don't forget our deal."

"Our deal?" He looks to me, the fine lines around his eyes crinkling the way I love.

"The one we just made, my sexy husband. I promise to love you forever..."

"And I'll never let you go." He smirks. "Not even if you beg."

"So now you're going to make me beg?" I tease as we slip into the barn and are greeted by a chorus of cheers.

Waving to our family and friends, we make our way to the head table, and Brooks leans down and whispers in my ear, "Only when you're naked."

"Can't wait," I say, finding us each a glass of champagne and holding mine up to his. "Cheers to us."

Brooks clinks his glass to mine. "Cheers to the best fucking deal I ever made."

EPILOGUE
RIDGE

"I can't believe they expect their guests to use an outhouse." Chastity stares at herself in the vanity mirror of my truck, puckers her lips, and reapplies her lipstick for the hundredth time tonight.

"They're called port-a-potties, and they ordered them in so that the whole damn town wasn't trampling through their house."

"Well, it's disgusting."

"So you mentioned, which is why I drove you all the way over to our ranch just to use the facilities."

My hint for her appreciation is ignored. Then again, so is my sour attitude. Guess I shouldn't hope for much more than that, but this woman's sky-high expectations are already getting on my nerves, and we haven't even said *I do* yet.

She pops the top back on the tube of lipstick and turns to me with an expression I think's supposed to be sultry but ends up looking more like she's got a bad case of gas.

"Well?"

Fuck, what have I forgotten now?

She fluffs her sleek platinum hair with manicured fingers that have never seen a day of work. The pale locks fall back perfectly into place, framing a face so heavily made-up, I'm not sure I even know what she looks like under all the layers.

I stare a moment, trying to come up with an answer to her vague as fuck question, but she's having none of it. In a huff, she asks, "Don't you want to tell me how nice I look?"

Chastity is not an ugly woman—far from it. She's beautiful, at least in the conventional sense, and I know a lot of men would bend over backward to have her at their side. But there's something about her—or maybe something wrong with me—I can't even fake an attraction.

And I'm sure as hell not gonna stroke her ego on command.

"Nope."

I hop out of the truck to avoid the backlash from my insult. She'll get over it, and the sooner she learns I won't pander to her, the better.

We may be getting married, but I'm not handing over my balls.

Still, I was raised to be a fucking gentleman, so I step around to the passenger side and open her door, offering her my hand.

Poised and seemingly unaffected by my behavior, she gingerly places her fingers in mine and exits the truck as though she were a starlet gracing a red carpet.

The Monroe barn is lit up like a Christmas tree and

bursting with activity. Loud music and rowdy townsfolk beckon us from the doorway.

But before we make it there, Chastity turns on me, stopping me dead in my tracks, pointing one of her painted talons at my chest.

"We're going in there, you're going to dance with me, and you're going to do it with a smile on your face. You will be polite and act like you're happy to be here. Got it?"

Well, she's ballsy, I'll give her that.

"And if I don't?"

"I don't have to marry you, you know. It's not like you're my only option." She leans into me, taunting. "But your mother explained exactly what this marriage means for you and how much she supports it. Maybe you should keep that in mind."

Ah yes, Mama.

The woman in charge of it all. For now.

Not only has she demanded I get married, fulfilling the stipulation of Pa's will, but she's gone as far as picking my goddamn bride-to-be. I know she's grieving, and only wants what's best for me, but it doesn't make this shit any easier.

The worst part is there's nothing legal about the supposed clause, and there's no reason I need to be married to run the ranch. It's just more of Pa's head games.

Although, I wouldn't be surprised if Mama gave him the idea to begin with. As much as she loves her family, she does have a ruthless side—one she taught me well.

She wants me tied down because she's anxious for me to have kids. Not that she cares about grandbabies—for a woman who raised nine of us, she's not that maternal. It's more about shaping the next generation, and continuing the legacy of the Kincaide name.

At least I know how to handle her. Not like my brother, Brooks. He never knew how to go along to get along or how to work her whims to his benefit. There's a fine art to manipulation—especially when it comes to Mama—but that's something Brooks just never learned.

Although it seems he made out all right, despite everything.

Head bowed and hands on my hips, I don't grace Chastity with an answer. I simply follow her into the throngs of the party.

Tables draped in white linens line the walls, streamers hang from the rafters, and the floor is covered in confetti. It looks like a party supply store blew up in here, and even though it's not the kind of shindig I'd typically enjoy, I can't help but smile.

Cheers erupt from the crowd, and I turn to see the bride and groom standing in the doorway. Brooks's smile is wider than I've ever seen, and Addie looks ready to burst with delight. She's the all-natural girl next door and not at all my type, but I can't deny Brooks lucked out when he found her.

"Well, are you going to ask me to dance?" Chastity prods from beside me.

A sharp stab of jealousy twists my gut as I watch my brother lean down and kiss his wife. She throws her arms around his neck, unconcerned about appearances or how many eyes are on them. Together they radiate a kind of love I'll never have.

But that's okay. I've got control of Canyon Spring Ranch. And Chastity's not the worst.

"I don't dance," I tell her. Then, deciding to see how far I can push things, lean down and whisper in her ear, "But if you're up for it, there's lots of private spaces on this property where I could show you my other moves. I'm pretty skilled with my hands and hips."

The look on her face lets me know I've definitely gone too far. Raising my hands, I chuckle, "Just teasing. C'mon, let's hit the dance floor."

I lead her out to the center of the barn where couples twist and turn to an upbeat tempo. I'm surprised when, despite the obvious stick up her ass, she jumps right into the mix, keeping time and allowing me to spin her around.

Maybe there's hope for us to get along, after all.

Her long, graceful arms wind their way up my neck as the music slows to a more romantic beat. She leans into me, her small but firm tits pressing into my chest.

Yeah, I could get used to this.

"I hope you don't always plan to be so rude and crass," she murmurs through a smile. "What would people think if they'd heard you?"

Shit, this woman has no idea who I really am. Then again, does anyone?

The way I was raised, the life I've lived—in constant competition for not only my livelihood but my father's affection—I've never had the luxury of letting my guard down long enough for anyone to know me.

Except maybe that one time—that one glorious night

and the one delectable fucking woman I still can't get out of my head. My one and only one-night stand. Lacy.

Hell, I may never dispel the thoughts of her hooded eyes, wild, sweat-soaked hair, and the sounds she made with her head thrown back in ecstasy as she came around my cock... *fuck.*

I grit my teeth, urging my body not to betray me. The last goddamn thing I need is for Chastity to think her bitchy attitude makes me hard.

We continue dancing—she's too close for comfort—and I look around for something, anything, to take my mind off the unwanted friction of her body.

But then the crowd parts slightly and I see her.

Lacy.

Except it can't fucking be. There's no way in hell she'd show up here.

I shake my head, trying to force away her image.

But with another twirl around the room, she's there again. Only this time, those dark eyes capture mine and hold tight.

I twist my head, not wanting to lose sight of her, still not trusting she's really here.

But she is.

And her timing couldn't be fucking worse.

*T*hank you for reading The Cowboy Bargain. Next in the Canyon Spring universe is Ridge's story in The Cowboy Hitch. Available at major retailers in ebook and paperback. Grab it here www.smwestauthor.com or here www.kimberlyquinnbooks.com.

Thank you for reading and please leave a review on your favorite book site, including tell a friend. Reviews help readers find books!

ABOUT THE AUTHORS

S.M. WEST

USA TODAY bestselling and award winning author, S.M. West writes sexy, angsty stories about brave hearts and wild love, including, more times than not, heart-pumping twists and turns.

Apart from her infinite love of books, she's a self-professed wine, chocolate, and travel junkie. When not writing or hanging with her family, she's usually talking to her characters (in her head) or planning her next adventure.

www.smwestauthor.com

For new releases, exclusive excerpts, giveaways and more, sign up for her newsletter.

KIMBERLY QUINN

Kimberly Quinn is a steamy contemporary romance author, born procrastinator, and grumpy hero lover. She enjoys lively conversations, usually with imaginary people, and can often be found daydreaming at work.

Her stories are set in adventurous small towns, filled with beautifully flawed, relatable characters, and have lots of heart, spice, and sometimes, a suspenseful twist.

When she's not busy writing, she can be found with a coffee in hand, dog at her side, and exploring the wilds of her hometown in Ontario, Canada... Or on her couch, getting lost in a good story.

www.kimberlyquinnbooks.com

Join Kimberly on her writing adventure and sign up to her newsletter!

www.ingramcontent.com/pod-product-compliance
Lightning Source LLC
Chambersburg PA
CBHW032252310726
48973CB00008B/2389